Human C

---

[1] As a measure of my incompetence, I feel I should point out the first problem with this book. It was meant to be called 'Chicken Brains', for reasons which should become obvious to you. I've committed to 'Human Chicken' now, so this will forever be The Book With The Wrong Name.

Foreword

This is a ridiculous story.

There are probably some serious and life-changing moral messages hidden within, and as the author I feel I should know where they are.

The fact that I don't means that I'm either a literary genius who writes subconscious masterpieces, or I'm an idiot.

The choice is yours.

I am not a poultry expert; there are a lot of chicken nuggets[2] in these pages, and most of them are probably bonafide facts, but they've essentially come from the internet and are in no way verified. If you look upon this work of fiction as a handbook for chicken husbandry then you are an absolute moron and should not be allowed out by yourself.

---

[2] Great pun, right? I presume you've worked out that I mean information about chickens, and not deep-fried bits of chicken...

Charlie.

Charlie was an egg, in the past sense of the word. Before he was a chicken, he was an egg and before that he was obviously a chicken. As we all know, the chicken-egg-chicken cycle goes on ad infinitum, or at least until the point where we can answer the age-old question of which came first.

Charlie knew that he was a chicken, which might seem perfectly ordinary… except it's not. Most animals are - to the best of our knowledge - just animals. They do their animal things in the way that their species knows best, and they survive. A sheep bleats and nibbles and follows and various other sheepesque things, but probably doesn't really know that it is a sheep and not, for example, a carrot. At some level, a sheep knows that a beetle is crunchy underfoot and a wolf is something to run away from, but it's hard to imagine that their thought processes are sophisticated enough to be able to elucidate the difference.

Charlie was a whole different kettle of fish. Charlie knew he was a chicken. He burst out of his egg prison and was already a sentient being with the neurological capacity of a human. This on its own was miraculous, considering that he had a brain the size of a haricot bean, but we all know that this isn't a textbook and there will be precisely zero actual science in the depths of these pages.

Charlie walked around in his coop and was astounded to realise that he knew the word for 'coop'. Or 'walk', for that matter. He saw what he assumed was his mother and 'ran' over to her for a hug, but it became abundantly clear that chickens cannot hug, because chickens do not have arms. He flapped in the general direction of his mother, and promptly fell over. His mother was - as would be expected - also a chicken. She was 100% chicken in fact, and totally oblivious to the fact that he was not behaving in the way that chickens are meant to behave. He tried several conversational openings with her, but the words in his head came out as an assortment of clucks; a talking chicken would be even more ridiculous than a sentient chicken.

Although he could think like a person, Charlie was constrained by a restrictive lack of limbs or language. He knew that there was a latch holding the coop closed but didn't have the appropriate body parts to grab it and lift it. He knew that the person heading towards the coop was a person, but did not have the appropriate vocal cords to be able to ask them for an escape plan. He could see that this would be a problem.

When this person opened the latch to the coop, dipped their head and clambered in to put some feed down, Charlie shot out through the open door and made a bid for freedom. In his head he was sprinting for cover so fast that nobody could possibly catch up. In reality, he had legs that were 1.5cm long and was swept up in less than 30 seconds. He pecked the hand of the person who caught him because he felt he had to make some kind of stand for all of chickendom, but the sole response was "you little bastard", closely followed by a brief period of being airborne before landing back in the coop with a gentle thud.

Plan A was an unmitigated failure, but Charlie inexplicably knew the whole alphabet and was already working on Plan B. Plan B involved stealth, guile and a very small head. Charlie's tiny head could just about squeeze through the bars and grab whatever was on the other side. He started gathering the leaves that had become pressed against the chicken wire, and weaving them together until he had a ball of something that looked like it might be natural. He squeezed underneath it, and waited by the door for feeding time. When the door opened, he very slowly crept out and parked just on the other side of the wire, disguised as a pile of leaves. Once the person had gone, he threw off his leaf jacket and did a little victory dance, which immediately lead to a second failed escape attempt. He had not factored in the role of the cat who lived on the farm, and who simply loved to gift cute fluffy things to its owners. With remarkable care, Spanky the cat gummed Charlie, plodded up the garden towards the house (despite Charlie's incomprehensible protestations) and deposited him at the feet of the person that Charlie by now recognised as The One With The Food.

Back in the hutch, Plan C was born.

I won't burden you with the details of plan C; suffice to say that it involved a trouser leg, and a worm like one Charlie had never seen before, and never wanted to see again.

Charlie was beginning to wonder whether the alphabet was long enough, because by the time he had got to Plan V, he had achieved nothing.

Plan W was his best yet, and capitalised on his knowledge of actual words. Using chicken food, he spelled out the word 'HELP' on the floor of the chicken coop, and waited for The One With The Food to come back. Sadly, although Charlie was able to think like a human, he was not able to think like a terribly clever human, and watched in despair as his family ate his message. Plan W.0 substituted chicken food for pebbles, but there weren't enough to write more than 'HE…'. Plan W.1 took a little longer to instigate, because it required Charlie to excavate 32 pebbles with a pair of tiny feet. He stockpiled them for days, then eventually laid them out in the correct form. He waited next to his plea for help, and stood motionless when the One With The Food arrived, while all the other chickens ran away.

The One With The Food may have seen the word, but something in his head probably knew that chickens can't write and therefore it was impossible. When your eyes see things that are impossible, they tend to look beyond what they're seeing to something more credible, and allow the real image to scuttle off to a metaphorical filing cabinet somewhere at the back of your brain. This is what happened, and the green thing that Charlie inexplicably knew was a Wellington boot crushed his cry for help. In fact it very nearly crushed Charlie too, but he did the chicken version of a commando-roll at the last second.

Plan W.2 was essentially the same as Plan W.1, but with more jumping up and down and cheeping. By Plan W.14, Charlie had developed some artistic flair and was beginning to decorate his message with leaves and feathers. To no avail; the boot came just the same.

By this time, Charlie was no longer quite so cute and fluffy, and his digging apparatus was larger and more effective. His message got more and more ostentatious, following a digging mission that was almost archaeological. He spelled out "Will you please let me out, you blind twat" in rocks, and waited patiently for feeding time.

Children, it seems, are more observant than adults, and more able to accept the incredible truths that the world throws at us. Instead of the normal giant foot, a new one arrived. It was much smaller, and was accompanied by a high-pitched voice which said "Daddy, what's a twat?" before chasing the birds around the coop with an insatiable enthusiasm that sent them clattering into all corners and destroyed the message before The One With The Food could understand why his daughter had asked such a peculiar question.

This was progress, albeit very gradual progress.

Charlie kept writing. Around the time that he became a fully grown chicken, The (New) One With The Food read the message, and tucked the chicken under his arm. Charlie had a taste of victory and even dared to feel smug. In his head, he smiled, but of course chickens do not have mouths so smiling was a physical impossibility.

Whilst Charlie was aware of the concept of a 'kitchen' and all of the appliances therein, he was simultaneously not aware of ever having seen or visited one. It was almost as though the acquisition of knowledge had happened by some weird process of osmosis[3], arriving in his head without going through the usual channels of experience or learning.

---

[3] I am aware that the scientists among you will already be formulating a complaint to the publisher regarding my lack of understanding of the true meaning of 'osmosis'. A proper author would spend hours researching their facts in order to suspend the reader's disbelief and all that jazz. I am an improper author and will therefore unceremoniously tell you all to fuck right off. Thanks.

The kitchen was well equipped, and Charlie sat patiently on a pristine worktop, waiting for something to happen. I can't imagine what be thought he was waiting for; a private jet? A deep and meaningful conversation? The Second Coming? Whatever it was, it never materialised. After some clattering, a large saucepan appeared, and Charlie was apparently being measured for size. At this point it dawned on the feathered fool that this was more Masterchef than Mastermind, and things were not looking up.

There was a door. It was closed. It had a cat-flap in it, which seemed like an attractive proposition to a chicken who has just realised that they will be best served with roast potatoes and stuffing.

Charlie leapt majestically[4] off the worktop and flew[5] towards the cat flap. After skidding stylishly on the tiled floor and thudding to a graceless stop at the foot of the door, he pushed his way through and out into the world. He knew that he wouldn't have long to get away, because The One With The Food would obviously work it out fairly quickly. There were trees, bushes, a car and a shed. He would be fighting a losing battle with the car because there was no way he would be able to reach the pedals. The bushes were too obvious, and the shed had a door. Trees. Trees had to be the answer. Can chickens climb? Of course they can't but perhaps he could improvise.

An unimaginative shout of "Chicken? CHICKEN!" filtered through the open kitchen window, which was enough to

---

[4] This is purely artistic license. There was absolutely nothing majestic about any of this.

[5] Also artistic license; chickens have the aeronautical properties of a brick, but with less purpose.

spur Charlie into action. With a combination of frantic (and largely ineffectual) flapping, beak action and imaginative foot placement, he managed to get himself high enough up in the tree that he was invisible to a prospective chicken-hunter.

The sun went down.

The sun came up again.

The ground was still a long way away to a chicken with zero flight capacity and an unexpected stroke of vertigo. Charlie shimmied towards the edge of his branch, hoping he might be able to jump from there to somewhere less high than the branch, but less low than the ground. Although Charlie was a sentient being, he was not a sentient being who understood physics. In particular, he didn't understand gravity, and the elastic properties of wood. The portly feathered fool noticed that the ground was getting closer but wasn't fully aware of how to respond to this problem, or indeed whether it was even a problem. Surely reaching ground level so gently was a blessing?

No. It was not a blessing; it was simply an extended physics lesson.

As one foot stepped off the gently bending slender branch and onto the grass below, the shift in weight sent the branch flying back into the air, which in turn catapulted Charlie (who was still hanging on with his remaining foot) into orbit. Clearly he wasn't really 'in orbit', but he was travelling faster and higher than any chicken has any right to travel. When people say that their life flashes before their eyes in these situations, they are lying. Charlie thought something along the lines of "Whaaaaaarghghghh…" then landed. He did something close to bouncing, before waddling off in a direction that was neither 'house' nor 'hutch', nursing bruises on every part of his body.

The main problem with having the brain of a human but the body of a chicken, is that it is impossible to do any of the things that you think you ought to be able to do, and none of the words that are formulated in your head come out as actual words. Charlie could not get on a bus, but he knew what 'bus fare' was. He knew what a job was, but couldn't hold a pen to fill in an application form. Or do the job if he got it.

Over the next few hours, Charlie learned a lot about the shitshow of a life he was trying to navigate through.

He would get to a set of stairs and in his head he took them one at a time, but in real life he ran straight into them because his ridiculous legs weren't long enough. He saw people eating with shiny cutlery but himself had no choice but to eat by launching a full facial assault on the plate. He saw people dressed for a night out and briefly wondered how he would look if he wore what they were wearing, which was a futile use of grey matter given that he was a chicken. Chickens always look ridiculous in jeans, even if they're chicken-sized jeans. Jeans are just not chicken apparel. Cords perhaps; the stripes would complement the lie of the feathers beautifully. Khaki, maybe sage green.

Fashion quandaries were not exactly priorities in the circumstances, but it was nice to have a pleasant diversion from the agonies of thwarted expectation and face-planting flights of stairs[6].

---

[6] Actually, mostly individual steps, but that sounds way less cool and macho. Can a chicken even be macho?

As the internal comparisons between skinny and bootcut or stonewashed and block colour faded away and the chicken crossed the road[7], a fully laden truck driven by a texting man squealed around the corner. It is a proven fact that texting men (or women) make appalling drivers, and this particular Wayne was no exception. He saw the distracted Charlie too late and drove straight over him just moments after he saw him. Feeling immediately guilty, Wayne stopped and climbed down from the cab, only to see a confused Charlie sitting in the middle of the road with his feet splayed out in front of him. Wayne scooped him up and bundled him into the truck, ostensibly to check him over. It turns out that being a chicken has its' advantages; Charlie was much shorter than the bumper of the truck, and watched in terror as the underside of the truck swept overhead and what seemed like a hundred wheels whizzed by on either side.

Back on the road, Charlie was awarded a seat next to Wayne (mainly out of guilt) and shared a lunch of partially chewed crusts and crisp crumbs. He was hoping for doughnut crumbs too but every last crumb was cleansed from Wayne's hands by an energetic tongue. Every few miles, he hopped up and down enough to be able to see over the dashboard and work out where they were going. Since none of the place names were familiar, he gave up and made himself comfortable instead.

Some time later (difficult to wear a wristwatch when you have no wrists) Charlie was jolted back into consciousness by an aggressive speed bump, which lead to enthusiastic protestations from the rear of the truck. This was the first time that Charlie had even thought about what the truck might be carrying, and its contents were clucking wildly.

---

[7] There's a joke in there somewhere…

The speed bump was a harbinger of bad news.

They soon slowed down to a crawl, as colossal metal shutters clattered up in front of them, opening out into a dingy, cavernous room which echoed with some inexplicably harrowing noises. At first he couldn't tell what was happening in the gloom but once his brain caught up and joined up the dots, he figured out that it was the worst possible place for a chicken to be.

Wayne, it seemed, had grown to rather like Charlie, and as such Charlie felt that he was probably safe. From his vantage point on the dashboard, he surveyed the horrors before him.

Although sentient, it seems his knowledge of the meat industry was basic at best. The vista before him was therefore a huge shock to the system. He was in the poultry section, which would be the last sight that his chicken-buddies in the back would ever see. He watched, mesmerised as a batch of birds were prepared to meet their maker. They were loaded onto a conveyer belt in crates, and slowly passed through an enclosed box, and when they came out the other side they were no longer moving. The next part would give him nightmares for the remainder of his life.

The limp chickens were hung by their feet on a series of moving hooks. They passed through a bladed system which cut their heads clean off, then they moved out of sight. When the hooks re-emerged from their journey around the processing plant, they had no feet or feathers and their internal organs were all gone.

The whole process took just a few minutes and the contents of the crates seemed blissfully unaware of their fate. It was a constant stream of silent death and it made every feather on his body stand on end. Whilst he mentally filed this information, the truck was already being unloaded; his chicken-buddies would be nuggets by noon.

Wayne had left the window open[8] and after several embarrassing failed attempts, Charlie took a running jump and flapped high enough to get through the open window and nose-dive onto the slaughterhouse floor. He was smart enough to realise that a loose chicken in an abattoir would not be running around for long. He scurried across to the opening of the Killing Box and hid underneath.

At this point, Charlie realised that he could read, which was a stroke of good luck as it meant that he could read the "Emergency gas shut-off" sign. Looking back along the conveyor belt, he saw that the crates were held closed using a latch system that could easily be undone from the outside, but not from the inside. He hatched a dastardly plan suitably fast, foiled only by the fact that the gas shut-off button was higher than flapping-distance; he'd need something to press it with.

He wasn't strong enough to wield a broom or a mop, but there was a small piece of wood and a brick, which might be enough. He set up an elaborate see-saw system that looked like something from a computer game, climbed onto a chair, and jumped onto the see-saw. Poor aim thwarted his plan in the short term, but on his third attempt the brick moved. It didn't move far, but it moved a bit. He found a half brick instead, pushed it up to the see-saw like a rugby-

---

[8] Ironically, to keep Charlie alive.

chicken in training, and then prepared to leap again. This time it launched into low-earth orbit and completely missed the button.

It took six attempts but eventually the button was depressed[9]. A fresh batch of birds were being loaded, so Charlie needed to time the next part of his plan with military precision. As the first unsuspecting crate of birds got to the threshold of the Killing Box, Charlie's head bobbed up and he pecked the latch open with his beak. Seconds later his partners in crime would throw open their crate and make a bid for freedom

The next few crates sailed past and he bounced up like a messed-up Whack-a-Mole and unlatched them all. After six crates there was a lull as one of the men loading them had stopped to tie his laces. Charlie ran to the end of the Killing Box to see the freed chickens enjoy their first taste of freedom.

He had forgotten how incredibly stupid chickens are. They were still in their crates, looking as bemused as it's possible to look without eyebrows. They were just much less dead than the staff were expecting them to be, although the staff weren't that bright either because nobody seemed to have noticed.

An alternative and far more dastardly plan formed inside the supercharged chicken-brain.

There were 160 crates in total, and he systematically unlatched 140 of them before anyone noticed that there was a problem. Whilst the staff frantically tried to work out why

---

[9] We're talking 'pressed in' here rather than in need of psychological support. It's a button.

no birds had died for a while, Charlie threw open one of the crates and shouted "BOO!"[10] to the terrified creatures inside. They scattered on cue, and half flew, half ran and half fell[11] in every direction at once.

The ensuing chaos was enough to give him the time and space to start on all of the other crates. As each lid flipped open, the chaos increased exponentially; each member of staff trying to catch a chicken but there were less than 10 members of staff and around 1,600 birds. Whilst they tried to catch a second bird, they generally let go of the first, or had a face full of chicken and let go of everything. They stood on chickens, tripped over chickens, got pecked by chickens, got feathers up their noses and learned a whole array of expletives that they didn't even know they knew. The upshot was, that after twenty minutes of squawking and squealing, three people had hold of one chicken each, two were limping, one was unconscious, two had run away and the remaining two were sitting on the floor, back to back, in tears.

The remaining flock were roosting in the roof, on top of cars in the carpark, attempting to get into trees or just gratuitously crossing roads. 1597 chickens were causing havoc, and Charlie was overwhelmed with pride. But wait. What about the other three? With barely a thought for his own welfare, he put his 'fingers' in his mouth to whistle for some of his brethren to support his rescue attempt. Of course what actually happened was that he fell over, because toes were the closest he had to fingers, and he was standing on them. It didn't even make a whistling noise,

---

[10] It was more "SKRAAAAAAK" than "BOO" but the effect was the same.

[11] Yes, I am aware that this is really bad maths.

but it did make one of the men laugh so hard that he dropped his chicken.

The chicken thought very quickly (for a chicken) and flapped enthusiastically in the general 'groin' area of the man next to him, which shocked (or aroused) him so much that he too dropped his treasure. The two birds flanked the third man, made a strange gurgly noise and eyeballed the third man. They cocked their heads in unison and looked ready to charge. That was enough; the third man dropped his bird and ran away. He squealed like a stuck pig; the irony was not lost on Charlie.

So what next? Perhaps Charlie could be the King of the Chickens? He went out into the carpark and tried to round up some of the confounded fowl but it was - unsurprisingly - like herding chickens. Instead, he opted for startling them enough to make them run as far away as possible and hopefully live to cluck another day.

Charlie jumped/climbed up onto a wall and perched, feeling smug. In every direction, there were feathers and noises and a mixture of delight and confusion. Charlie had done something good and was ready for whatever life threw at him next.

Except he wasn't.

As he gazed into the middle distance, the man who had a shamefully erotic moment with a chicken just minutes earlier crept up from behind him (with gloves on) and grabbed an unsuspecting Charlie from his perch. Things took a very sudden turn for the worst, and Charlie did not have a plan B this time.

By this point, it was closing time and too late for all the machinery to be turned back on. Charlie was thrust unceremoniously into one of the many discarded crates, chucked onto the back seat of a car with leather seats, and driven away.

On principle, Charlie squeezed out the biggest shit he could muster onto the shiny seats. When the car went round a corner and the crate shifted, he shat again; if he was going to die then he would go out in flames.

By the time the journey was over, the back seat looked like a Jackson Pollock and a new array of expletives fell out of the driver's mouth. Charlie was bundled back out of the car and dropped in a corner of a dark room, surrounded by coats and shoes.

He needed to get out of the crate if he wanted to avoid paying the price of every single released bird. The crates were designed to be opened from the outside, but they were also designed for normal chickens. Charlie was not a normal chicken. Once he got accustomed to the gloom, he looked through the gaps in the crate for things that he could use to lever the latch off with. He found a clothes peg and - after extensive crate wiggling - a tent peg. Together they were enough, although he then discovered that he didn't have the leverage to open the lid from the inside, however open the latch might have been.

He was a portly bird, and was able to shift his weight suddenly enough to pitch the crate onto its side so that he could walk out like a cat through a flap. Problem 1 solved. Opening the door of the room he was in was a whole new challenge. It was a round doorknob that he would never be able to grasp; opening the door himself was apparently not an option.

Hanging up on a peg was a large handbag, which was clearly owned by a lady who liked to be Very Prepared. Inside, Charlie found 13 different pens, several hankies in varying stages of cleanliness, enough paper to write a novella, two pairs of socks and a catapult. There were other things too but Charlie had all the information he needed; there was enough space in the cavernous handbag for a well folded chicken.

The handbag did not smell nice. Charlie couldn't put his finger on what was offending his nostrils[12] but he figured a bad smell was better than certain death.

Indeterminate hours later, there were rumblings beyond the door, and Charlie burrowed further into the stench of the handbag into something squishy at the bottom of the bag.

The door opened.

Someone loud and shouty burst into what turned out to be the cupboard under the stairs, grabbed the bag, and left at pace.

Following the loud and shouty person was another loud and shouty person, but shouty at a considerably higher pitch and without any distinguishable words.

There were some bangs and clicks, Charlie's bag was thrown into what he assumed was a car, an engine started

---

[12] Yes. I am aware that chickens have neither fingers nor nostrils, We're talking figuratively again, folks.

and it felt like one step closer to freedom. Charlie dared to take a peek out of the bag.

Sticking his head up (in that typically chickenesque way, where they extend their necks like a feathered slinky) into the unknown, he found himself face to ~~face~~ beak with a live human baby, whose reflexes were astonishing. He (or she?) grabbed Charlie's beak with lightning efficiency and a squeal of delight.

Grabbing the confused chicken and shaking him about plenty before Charlie could react, the excitable infant continued to giggle and brought Charlie's face up towards his drooling face for what looked like a severe gumming. Using his back feet to grab the child's nose, Charlie was able to wriggle free and retreated under the passenger seat whilst the gyrating mountain of dribble descended into hysteria at the loss of its new toy.

Charlie knew that when the car stopped he would only have seconds to make his escape, and was ready to leap out of his sanctuary at any moment. Then the unthinkable happened. The bag that had been his escape route fell off the seat and landed in the passenger footwell, blocking his exit. Worse than that, he spotted the used nappy that he had been sleeping on. This is the point where he discovered that chickens cannot vomit. This was a strange sensation; his brain 'knew' that he felt nauseous, but his body didn't.

Now the only way to escape would be through the front door, but the passenger door wouldn't be opening, because there was no passenger. Could he pull the latch and open the door himself? No. Of course he couldn't. He was a chicken.

The only way out would be through the driver's door, or the baby's door. Charlie wasn't sure which was scarier; an adult who wasn't attached to their seat, or a teething baby.

The car stopped. Charlie went on his instincts. As soon as the door opened, he shot out from under the seat, flapped wildly in the poor woman's face until she batted him away like a bluebottle, and then flopped back onto the passenger seat. Not quite the escape he'd planned, but he wasn't dead so he was still winning.

Neither Charlie nor the woman with feathers up her nose knew what to do next. Looking suspiciously across at him, she edged her hand towards the car door. At no point did she take her eyes off him, and he was hypnotised by her hollow stare.

There was a click.

To his left, the electric window slowly lowered; she was clearly as wary of him as he was of her, and opted for granting him a safe exit that didn't involve her face. He used it, as gracelessly as a housebrick.

Once again, Charlie found himself in a car park. This one was punctuated by children making a variety of noises, and various people cooing. This made him nervous and his fight or flight instinct didn't know what to do with itself. This moment of indecision cost him dearly because once again he was plucked by an opportunistic stranger.

"Look! A chicken! The kids would love to see a chicken!"

Would they though? Would they really? Although how much harm could a room full of small children really do[13]? Not that he had a choice at this point, as he was tucked firmly under the arm of the person who announced him, and she had clearly done this before as she was holding his feet with her other hand.

By the end of the day, Charlie had 'worn' a hat, been dipped in jelly, dunked in a toilet and dressed in a nappy. Fortunately it was a clean one, which was an improvement on the morning's experience. He felt he had done his penance to the world, for the sins of an entire flock of mass murderers.

He left the building via another window, which was becoming a bit of a habit. This time he had the foresight to check what was on the other side of the window, and make something like a plan for what he'd do when he got there.

Charlie felt that he needed to put a lot of distance between him and anything that might cluck, shout, or shit itself. A handy pickup truck that was just pulling away seemed the perfect solution, and he crept underneath a tarpaulin to sit down and think about as little as possible.

Several hours later, Charlie made a mental note to never go to a casino. Luck was not something that seemed to be in his arsenal as the pickup truck belonged to a farmer and he parked it in a barn with no discernible exit. Perfect. In the distance, he heard the inimitable sound of clucking that would have brought tears to his eyes, if he had tear ducts.

---

[13] Apart from biting/gumming, pulling out his feathers, swinging him around by his feet, throwing rocks at him, sitting on him, poking his eyes out… Nothing really…

The average life expectancy for a chicken is around 7 years. At this point in Charlie's life this seemed literally impossible.

He was in a barn; the kind that tractors get stored in. It was made of corrugated metal, and had three tractors in it. There was some straw at one end and a massive (closed) door at the other. The floor was compacted soil and there were occasional drips from tiny holes in the roof. It was dark in the barn, and the holes looked almost like distant stars. If it hadn't been such a horrific situation, it might have been quite romantic.

A soil floor meant worms, so at least there was a food supply of some kind if the worst came to the worst. It was (mostly) dry, there was no wind and there were plenty of places to hide. He figured he could stay in the barn for the remainder of his 7 year life without coming to any harm, but that was not much of a life. He weirdly yearned for other chickens, but also knew that he hated avian company because he had a myriad of conversations in his head that he would never be able to have; not with any species. At least the chickens wouldn't be mainly trying to kill him, which was a bonus.

He started to dig. His claws were pretty sharp and his legs were strong, but it was taking forever to make any headway with the floor. The metal walls of the barn were sunken into the ground, and there was no way to know how far down he would have to dig. He felt like a prisoner trying to escape from a life sentence with nothing but a teaspoon to dig a ten mile tunnel with.

Charlie's three metre hole[14] had exhausted and frustrated him in equal measure and there was literally no light at the end of the tunnel. He was trying to ignore the fact that there wasn't even a tunnel.

At this point, Charlie revisited an earlier plan that he had discounted as a ridiculous idea. He was still a chicken, and his abilities still revolved around that fairly significant fact. There were still a million things that were beyond him as a result of his physical makeup, but he also still had the same awareness of the things in the world that he probably couldn't actually do but knew the theory of. He knew the theory of how to make a cup of tea, how to write a letter and - significantly - how to drive.

The pickup truck was parked tantalisingly just behind him, the keys left in the ignition and dangling free. Was there a reality in which he could use the pickup to escape somehow? In practical terms, he couldn't both press the clutch and accelerator because he feet were too short. He also couldn't both use the pedals and change gear or indeed look out of the windscreen. Putting all of this together, the concept of driving seemed a bridge too far.

Or possibly it was just a problem that needed solving. Charlie liked problems, in the same way as a genius mathematician might. Whilst he loved the idea of comparing himself to the likes of Pythagoras and Alan Turing, he was also acutely aware of the fact that even couldn't even operate a calculator.

Since the door was an actual barrier to getting into the car, it was a massive blessing that the window was open. Charlie

---

[14] Closer to 3 centimetres, but a valiant effort.

fluttered energetically into the car and surveyed the situation. This clarified his previous assertion that he wouldn't be able to drive, because - frankly - he wouldn't be able to drive.

Turning the key was probably an option, and so were all of the other components of driving, just not simultaneously. There just weren't enough available limbs. On closer inspection, it transpired that Charlie wasn't heavy enough to press the pedals, and his beak wasn't big enough to grip the gearstick, but he could almost grasp it with a foot. The pedals were the next hurdle. He could get a brick and put it on one of the pedals like they do in the movies, but he wasn't strong enough to carry a brick. Even if he was, he wouldn't be able to co-ordinate this with changing gear because the gearstick was too far away from the pedals.

Added to that there was the tiny detail that the pickup truck was facing the wrong way; he'd have to reverse out. According to the diagram on top of the gearstick, reverse meant pressing a button on the side of the gearstick which was a long way from possible.

A stick. A stick would solve one problem. Like an underfluffy and misshapen dog, Charlie found a stick. He wedged the stick between the clutch and the seat so that the clutch was in. This was an excellent start.

A small pebble. That would solve a second problem, if combined with some elastic. After rifling around in the cab of the pickup truck, Charlie found the most rancid pair of underpants he had ever seen. He wasn't sure that he'd seen a lot of underpants, but the rainbow of stains in this pair was definitely in the category of 'rancid'[15]. Using his beak with a great deal of trepidation, he ripped the elastic out of the underpants and flicked the remainder as far out of the window as he could manage with his feet. He then skilfully wrapped the elastic around the gearstick, so that it held a small pebble in place, pressed against the little button on the side. With some flapping and wriggling and pressing and an almost catastrophic bum incident, he moved the stick. Now he had a pickup truck in reverse.

Problem 3 involved turning the key in the ignition and then accelerating. As the clutch was jammed in place, this was going to be a sudden and brief driving experience. Charlie limbered up by using the handbrake as a pommel horse and the steering wheel as some not-at-all-parallel bars. It was time. From the headrest of the seat, he thrust himself at the steering wheel, spun round underneath it, turned the key as he passed it and then threw himself at the accelerator as the car lurched backwards. He was essentially going full throttle backwards through a massive metal door into what he hoped was a farmyard. Beyond that was a mystery.

Obviously he fell off his 'perch' on impact, and was astounded to discover that - despite its age - the pickup truck was in fact fitted with the full complement of airbags. The initial impact set off the one in the steering wheel, which caught him on the side of the head and sent him sprawling against the window on the passenger side. Hitting the barn caused a pile of empty oil cans to fall over and hit the side of the truck, which in turn set off the side impact airbags. This thrust him back towards the driver's side, but the first airbag hadn't deflated yet, so he got caught in a comedy

---

[15] It was a miracle that he never wondered why there were manky pants in the truck. The vile reality would have been too much.

situation where he was bounced between partially inflated airbags. He might have found it funnier if his brain wasn't vibrating.

The collision had made what might be politely described as 'a bit of a racket', so escaping before anyone arrived seemed like a good plan. He climbed out of the window and landed like a person who had drunk their own weight in tequila. He might have bounced; he wasn't sure. After something more like a roll than a walk into a bush, he sat down and contemplated his life.

His contemplations didn't get much further than whether chickens could get concussion. An indeterminate amount of time later, Charlie answered his own question by realising that he had been unconscious and had the mother of all headaches.

And he was really hungry.

He was responsible for finding his own food, which was new. He had the brain capacity of a person, and apparently lacked the instincts of a chicken. He knew that he should probably fancy eating something which either had no legs or at least six, but his human brain was yearning for a cooked breakfast and a glass of orange juice[16].

There was a house. On the one hand, houses contain food. On the other hand, they contain people, saucepans and really big knives. Clearly being gutted and boiled was worse than being a bit hungry, but apparently being hungry makes ~~people~~ chickens do really stupid things. Five minutes later, Charlie was teetering on the edge of a very slippery

---

[16] He was acutely aware that if he tried to drink a glass of orange juice, he would probably drown.

windowsill and leaping hopefully at an open window that he wasn't certain he would fit through. Bad plan. Do people leave back doors open? No, it turned out. Could he jump onto the handle of the door and open it? Also no. Could he sit on the floor and sulk like a teenager in a power cut? Yes. Definitely yes.

When a car pulled up, Charlie snapped out of his sulk and hid in another bush. From out of the car came two People, both of whom carried large plastic bags which were absolutely rammed with food items that would have made Charlie salivate if that was in any way possible for a chicken. The People put their bags down and returned to the car, whereupon one of them noticed that the barn was partially demolished and the car had escaped. They both ran off wailing, leaving Charlie in grocery heaven. There was corn on the cob, crisps, fresh bread, breakfast cereal, chocolate and shampoo. The shampoo gave Charlie a strange sense of nostalgia for hair that he felt like he had once had. Shampooing feathers was impossible for so many reasons; no fingers to work up a lather with for a start.

Back in reality, the hungry chook had a moment of clarity and stockpiled an assortment of delectables for a repast at some point in the future. Then he dove into a giant bag of crisps like it was the first time he had ever eaten in his life. Hearing the People return to their shopping from the inside of the crisp packet was bad news, because he was trapped. He tried to grab the packet and pull it up over his head, and remembered (again) that he had no hands; he fell over instead. This left him in the unenviable position of being upside-down in a half full bag of crisps, with rapidly encroaching People who would not appreciate his situation, or the trail of sweetcorn kernels in his wake.

He drew up his feet into the family-sized bag and hoped for the best.

After the People had finished wringing their hands and discussing a variety of scenarios which might have lead to the carnage before them, they starting clearing up. The eruption of a Charlie from his bag haven gave one unsuspecting farmer's daughter such a fright that she threw it up in the air. Being in the air made his 'bird' instincts come to the surface, and he flapped like his life depended on it[17]. This was fairly ineffectual, because he was inside a plastic bag. All he achieved was to frighten the girl even more, such that she started batting at the air like she was trying to fly herself, swiping poor Charlie out of the sky and driving him into the ground. Dazed and thoroughly confused (for the second time), Charlie reversed out of the bag and scuttled away.

'Away' seemed like a good place to be, and Charlie carried on scuttling until he was as 'away' as he could manage without a rest. When the rest came, it was at the side of what would be described in poetry as a 'babbling brook'. It was calming and gentle, with the occasional fish passing through and a host of water-boatmen and dragonflies. His inner human marvelled at the beauty of it all. His inner chicken wondered how many dragonflies he could fit in his mouth at once. He didn't have an inner dog, but if he did, it would have been planning a mud bath.

It was cold and increasingly dark. Charlie felt exposed by himself on the riverbank, and an urge to nest took him by surprise. He found bits of grass, some stray magpie feathers and dried leaves, and wove them together at the base of a

---

[17] There was a distinct possibility that it actually did.

hedge. His nest was big enough to snuggle into and before he'd even finished thinking about a soft duvet that he almost maybe remembered, he was asleep.

The sun came up[18] and Charlie woke up and yawned. 'Yawned' is a bit of a stretch though as the noise that came out was nothing like what he was sure a yawn was meant to sound like.

"Cooorkuhduddldaaargh!"

He even surprised himself with the syllables that were warbling out of his throat. He felt like an opera singer but with more feathers and considerably fewer discernible words[19]. He manoeuvred onto a branch slightly higher up and had another go.

"Cockadoodledoooooo!"

It felt like this was a noise he was born to make, but the person in him felt ridiculous. The chicken in him puffed out its chest and took a deep breath before blasting out a third call. He was announcing his chickenness to the world; telling the world how much of a cock he was. The more he shouted, the more natural it felt and the more he wanted to shout. In the branches above him, his announcement was heard; smaller birds scattered amidst the boom of his voice. In the grass below him, his call was heard; mice leapt out of their holes and shot across the field behind him, in fear of

---

[18] It has a habit of doing that.

[19] Charlie wasn't totally sure that this was true. He had fairly limited experience of opera but it all seemed like multisyllabic warbling to him. This was largely because he didn't understand a word of Italian beyond 'pizza'.

their lives[20]. In a bush just next to him, his call was heard; a very quiet fox leapt out of the bush and took him by the throat. Charlie stopped announcing things.

---

[20] In all honesty it was more that he sounded awful than that he was in any way scary. Very little about a chicken is scary.

Henrietta

Henrietta was an egg. She obviously didn't know that she was an egg, because she was an egg and eggs are not renowned for their thinking. Henrietta was one of five, snuggled up together in a nest in the corner of a wooden hutch at the end of a garden.

Henrietta wriggled because that was all she could really do. She felt like she was jammed into a tiny space[21] and all she wanted to do was stretch. Every instinct in her wanted to stick out her neck and stretch out her legs. It was almost primeval. Those of us who are not eggs know that this is exactly what normally happens with chickens in eggs but Henrietta had very little experience of the whole egg-hatch-egg cycle. In fact, in her minuscule chicken brain, she was human. She had half-memories of crisps and cars and nappies, and lived in the body of a chicken. This was confusing to her already, and she hadn't even hatched yet.

At the point of hatching, Henrietta felt like she was really badly hungover. As a chicken, heavy drinking is a peripheral concern at best. It falls well behind a myriad of other issues:

1. Do I have food?

2. Is there a fox?

3. Where are my eggs?

4. Is it raining?

5. Is that a fox?

---

[21] That's exactly what she was.

6. Do I have food?

7. How do I get up there?

8. Why does my bum[22] hurt?

9. Can I eat this?

10. What's that noise?

11. Does that smell like a fox?

12. Why is that bird attacking me?

...and considerably further down the list...

426. Eurgh, when will this hangover go away?

On this occasion, Henrietta just wanted to stretch out and get some fresh air. She pushed out her tiny feet, stretched her neck, and felt the satisfying crack of her eggshell prison. Out popped her head, like a submariner starting shore leave. She stood up and swiftly 'remembered' the principles of physics that she couldn't possibly ever have learned[23] as she fell over, simultaneously revisiting both gravity and balance as she flopped helplessly onto the floor. Only one leg had escaped. This was a problem as it was apparently impossible to balance without a full set.

She stretched again, and... Crack.

---

[22] Chickens don't have bums, they have cloacas. Or possibly cloaci. Most chickens don't know this though, because they're chickens. They certainly don't know the etymology of 'cloaca' nor indeed the concept of etymology.

[23] ...because she was a chicken!

Two legs. Now Henrietta looked like a caricature of herself, with two legs out of the bottom of her shell and fragments of it still stuck to her comically fluffy baby feathers. She waddled around for a while, aware that she could easily be the star character in a child's television series. Her waddling led her into a lump of wood, which was followed by another 'crack' and then the freedom of the rest of her body.

Before she had even managed to catch up with what was going on in her life, another chicken a thousand times larger than her bore down on her like a steam train. It squawked in a way that would scare a human half to death but would presumably reassure a baby chicken. After a brief and fruitless chase around the hutch, Henrietta ascertained that this was almost certainly her mother, who was trying to do the chicken equivalent of putting her to bed with a story and a blanket. The 'story' was a sequence of horrific high pitched noises and the 'blanket' was a combination of hay and feathers. To a chick this was probably bedtime perfection, but to someone who's used to 14 togs and Egyptian cotton, it was not ideal. Henrietta hadn't quite got her head around this weird limbo in which she existed, where she was neither one nor the other. Chicken in body, person in mind. Neither quite seemed to fit.

Amid loud and very confused protestations, Henrietta and her fellow chicks were herded back to the heap of hay that was apparently 'bed'. It was much more comfortable than anticipated, and - when engulfed by a flock[24] of chicks, it was really quite warm and snuggly. Henrietta wiggled her bum around until the straw under her was Henrietta-shaped, folded her tiny wings in and drifted off to sleep. To anyone else, this would have seemed an impossible task. During the day, chickens are responsible for a fairly consistent

---

[24] It was probably more of a 'brood' than a 'flock' but to a very tiny chick it felt like there were a billion other chickens in the vicinity.

cacophony of clucking, squawking and occasional screeching. To a person, this would not be conducive to a restful night, but presumably to a chicken it is a comforting sound. Who knows; perhaps there's intellectual conversation amongst the clucking.

Henrietta's inner person, however, found the noises irritating and downright alarming, so she woke up after a very short period of time. She was hungry. She had dreamed of chocolate fudge cake and roast potatoes, lasagne and crumble[25]. It quickly became clear that none of these things were on this particular a la carte menu. There was no silver service, no serviettes, no cruet and not even a hint of cutlery. In fact all that was on offer was worms. Warm, still wriggling, worms. Pink, probably quite squelchy and almost certainly earthy. Worms.

At this point, Henrietta was experiencing a strange mix of emotions. Like Charlie before her, she was simultaneously exuberant and repulsed. Her chicken instincts made her extend her tiny little neck as much as she could so that she got the juiciest worms, whilst her human instincts retched at the prospect. In her head she was ordering a pizza with a side order of cheesy garlic bread. Maybe some potato wedges and perhaps a bottle of something hideously sweet and wind-inducingly fizzy. Whilst she salivated at the prospect of eight triangles of stuffed crust, she was actually already swallowing the worms being thrust down her throat by a loving mother.

Gorged on invertebrate goodness, Henrietta settled down into a glorious fuzz of unconsciousness. She woke up when her human brain remembered that the sounds around her were really obnoxious and not as soothing as her chicken brain had thought. Her siblings had already scarpered and were bounding around the coop like they hadn't a care in

---

[25] Not all at once.

the world[26]. She did not have the urge to join in with their wild chirping and frolicking, and was quite happy to participate as a spectator. She tucked her ridiculous wings in and watched what was happening around her with a metaphorically raised eyebrow[27].

As she watched from her corner, a real human-shaped person walked towards the coop with a bucket full of food. It was a young man, and the first thing he noticed was the incongruous Henrietta, sitting serenely in the corner, while chaos reigned around her. He bent his head so that he could fit through the door, and came in with his bucket. The other fowl scattered to any part of the coop that separated them from the boy, but Henrietta stood (or sat) her ground. For a while, they had the world's least equitable staring competition[28]. Then the young man scooped Henrietta up with an audible "Awwwww!" and popped the adorable ball of fluff into the pocket of his duffel coat[29]. Henrietta squeaked.

After several uncomfortable hours (which involved cutting a hedge, changing a tyre, taking an unfeasibly large dump and a period that Henrietta struck immediately from her memory) in that pocket, Henrietta was eventually released into the bedroom of the boy, who turned out to be called Dan.

---

[26] In all fairness, they really had no cares in the world.

[27] Chickens don't have eyebrows.

[28] Chickens have three eyelids. The one closest to the eyeball is essentially see-through, so when they blink they don't even really blink. Or perhaps they do, but they never fully blink. Or maybe they constantly blink. Either way, it certainly wasn't fair for Henrietta to be in a staring contest with someone with normal blinking capacity.

[29] Duffel coats always seem to have pockets big enough for an encyclopaedia Brittanica. Not that most wearers of Duffel coats are particularly enthusiastic about carrying encyclopaedias around with them, but the principle is what matters here.

Because Henrietta thought like a person, she made an excellent house guest. When she needed to relieve herself, she tapped on the window. Dan opened the window and she hung her bum over the edge and let rip. She tucked herself in next to him in bed when the lights went out, which only became a problem if she turned around in her sleep and poked him in the eye with her beak. While she still had baby feathers, she was really soft against his face, which he found really comforting; like a self-warming hot water bottle.

As she got older and more like a chicken, she was less fluffy but larger and therefore warmer to curl up with. She was strong enough to pick up the clothes that Dan left strewn around on his floor and deposit them in the linen basket. She perched on his shoulder while he read at night, woke him up gently in the morning and expertly massaged his back with her feet. It was a match made in heaven.

And then things got weird.

Like most people, Dan had a routine; he got up, took his clothes into the shower, and came back clean and dressed. At the end of the day, he did a short workout, repeated his shower regime in reverse, and then went to bed.

On this particular sunny day, Dan broke ranks and did something different. He was tired, and couldn't be bothered to do his workout late at night. Instead, he got changed in the bedroom, right in front of Henrietta. There was, briefly, a real naked body in the room, and it was waggling and jiggling right in front of her. Her adult chicken brain couldn't get beyond "yummy worm" but her teenage human brain was tingling in a way that she simply didn't have the words for. Dan had been a good companion; he'd fed her, kept her warm and made her feel safe. He had talked to her, and they had started playing games together; hide and seek and a version of musical statues that mainly involved dancing[30]. They had grown quite close, as much as a person and a chicken (who thinks they're a person) can. She had never realised that he was attractive before.

This was information that she did not know how to process.

In time, Henrietta realised that she was staring. This was compounded by the fact that Dan had also realised that she was staring. Under normal circumstances, he would probably have turned away and protected his modesty, but this was a chicken. Why be embarrassed in front of a chicken? Instead of turning away, he did the reverse. He got closer to Henrietta and started gyrating in her general direction, in a way that no teenage boy should be able to master so effectively.

Henrietta was torn between dancing with him, and taking a huge bite. Before she could finish that particular thought process, she was spared the decision and the tasty worm was safely tucked away into some mercifully loose underpants. Henrietta flapped up to her roosting spot on the curtain pole, and began processing.

In the morning, Henrietta did something on the edge of romantic, and quietly got some clothes out for Dan. This was no mean feat; the jeans were in a closed drawer and the socks were tightly rolled up in a ball. For one peculiar minute, Henrietta had her head stuck in a jeans pocket and one foot in the pointless little top pocket of a blue t-shirt[31]. She carefully dragged the whole ensemble into the creepily posed shape of a person on the floor, pulling out the

---

[30] A chicken dancing is truly a thing to behold. There are a lot of feathers and general flapping, coupled with vigorous foot movement. The presence of music is almost irrelevant because chickens have no sense of timing, apparently.

[31] It may or may not have been blue. Chickens are, after all, colourblind.

wrinkles with increasingly skilful claws and an unacceptably damaging beak that perforated more items of clothing than perhaps Dan would appreciate.

When Dan dragged his stinky skinful of hormones out of bed, he tripped over the expectant bird at the foot of his bed and fell into the beautifully laid out outfit on his floor, runkling[32] it up into a pile that made it look like clothes he'd discarded the night before. There was a split second in which he was confused and couldn't remember having worn those clothes for ages, but this was so brief that you'd miss it if you blinked. Then, in an ignorantly thoughtless gesture, he kicked them into the corner and went off to the toilet. The human part of Henrietta's messed up brain wanted to claw out his eyes, and her poultry parts just wanted to poo. In a poetic combination of emotions, she pooed vindictively and systematically on every item of clothing she could find. The She shuffled them around like a reverse avian washing machine to ensure that she spread her excrement around a significant portion of wall and floor. When she stepped back to admire her handiwork, there was an immediate surge of guilt, followed by a vain attempt to clear it up. 'Clearing it up' translated into spreading it around even further, so Henrietta did the only thing her chicken instincts had left.

She hid under the bed and kept very still indeed.

Dan came back, said lots of angry words that Henrietta didn't understand, kicked stuff around a bit and then threw all of his filthy clothes into a bin in the corner. In so doing, he also spattered a small amount of goop up the wall by the bin, and then said some more very angry words. Henrietta would have gasped as her innocence was wrenched from her, if she had understood a single expletive as it fell out of Dan's mouth.

---

[32] This is not a word.

Once dressed, Dan waltzed down the path below his bedroom window on his way to school. Henrietta contemplated corn. She wasn't person enough to understand the concept of heartbreak, but her stomach was well attuned to the concept of hunger. A combination of flapping and walking took her down to the kitchen, where she expertly[33] poured herself a bowl of dry cornflakes. It was a blessing for all concerned that she used a light melamine bowl, and could therefore get it to the sink without disaster. When she lost her grip, it just bounced a few times on the tiles and spread cornflake crumbs everywhere. This was all impressive for a chicken; even a really embarrassed one who's just smeared shit everywhere.

Henrietta carefully poked her head out through the cat flap in the kitchen door, surveyed the scene for the elderly (but still menacing) cat, and scrambled outside. She was missing Dan but didn't understand exactly what the emotion coursing through her was. She had another poo, in the hope that it would assuage her emotions. It didn't particularly make her feel better, but the brief moment of concentration refocused her brain and she forgot everything that had just happened. She started looking for worms instead and then began her one-chicken mission to eradicate the world (or at least the lawn) of invertebrates.

Dan, on the other hand, had a longer attention span than an average chicken, and was a long way away from forgiveness when he returned home. When Henrietta ran at him for a customary homecoming greeting cuddle, he hoofed her away like a deflated football. She had no idea what was going on as she could only remember back as far as worm #26 and just knew that she liked Dan. She then

---

[33] These things are all relative. For a chicken, 'expertly' in this context refers to the cornflakes mostly being in the bowl, and the bowl remaining intact for the duration. It was as 'expert' as a 3 year old's attempt might be, but at least the portion size was smaller.

tried to do that thing that happy cats do, and weaved in a figure of 8 around Dan's legs. When cats do this, it's lithe and flowing, their sleek bodies rubbing lovingly against an unsuspecting leg. When chickens do this, it's a ridiculous outpouring of feathers and legs that have the dexterity of a brick and a demeanour to match. This invariably ends in an interaction between face and floor, and today was no exception. Dan fell over. This did not improve his mood. He shouted "CASSEROLE" at Henrietta in a tone of voice that could only be described as threatening, and slammed the kitchen door in her face.

Henrietta knew that their relationship had broken down, and she knew that she needed to apologise. She also had a vague recollection of an extensive worm incident the night before that made her feel uncomfortable when she looked at Dan's groin. Fortunately, his groin was quite high up, and she was quite low down; looking at his groin took a lot of effort and was easily avoided. She flapped back inside and half flew, half jumped up the stairs to 'knock' on his bedroom door. There was grunting in his bedroom that she really couldn't quite fathom, so she waited patiently. The grunting got louder until it reached a crescendo, and was followed by silence. She knocked again (with her beak, obviously).

When he answered the door, Dan was clearly on his way to the shower as he was only in his underpants. He must also have suffered from a short-lived cold, as there was a heap of tissues on the floor next to the bed. Henrietta immediately set about collecting them all up in her beak and depositing them near the bin. She would have put them **in** the bin if she could, but it was still full of clothes. Dan watched her with a bemused expression, and then laughed. Henrietta understood laughter; it tended to mean happiness. She clucked over and rubbed gently against Dan's leg, and he scooped her up under his arm and made her comfortable on the bed next to him as he played on his phone. She went to sleep and woke up still next to him, but in horizontal form. She opened her eyes and looked at him as he dribbled and muttered his youthful fantasies in his dreams. She gently moved the hair off his forehead so she could see him better, and some strands of hair got into her throat. This lead to mild choking and she coughed so hard that she was sick on his face. This was a second lesson in failed romance, rescued only by the fact that Dan was a heavy sleeper, who wiped his face and rolled over. Henrietta went back up to her roost, unconsciously certain that this was best for everyone.

Let's be clear, Dan liked having Henrietta around because he didn't have many friends. He had absolutely no romantic feelings towards her at all, but a strange fondness for her that made him invite her under the duvet at night. He would definitely miss her if she wasn't there, but he didn't want to arrange a candlelit dinner for two with her, or take her on a romantic trip down the Seine. He kept her safe and she kept him company. That was all.

Henrietta was now one and a half, and very much full grown. Dan was 15 and very much a teenage boy. He was changing, and she was still just a chicken. If she was a bit more of a person, she might have had to make some difficult decisions at this point. The next day in school, Dan made a step towards adulthood, and asked a girl out. An actual girl, with no feathers, no habits of shitting in clothes, and a tendency to eat cornflakes with milk. And a spoon. She acquiesced[34] to his advances, which was the beginning of the end for Henrietta. He stopped wanting bedtime chicken warmth, and stopped coming home so quickly after school. Henrietta knew that she was seeing him less but obviously had no idea why until the day that he brought her home for 'tea'.

---

[34] A much underused word.

she heard them coming, Henrietta 'flew' up onto the the wardrobe, where she could hide in the shadows. ..as an instinctive action because she had absolutely no idea what was going on, but had a clear sense of 'stranger danger'. From her perch on the wardrobe she saw things that she would never be able to unsee. She saw the worm become a snake, and she watched it disappear. She heard noises that may have been happy or may have been angry; she couldn't tell which. The visitor had Henrietta's space on the pillow and it wasn't fair. Henrietta wasn't warm enough and she wanted her boy back. She jumped. She flapped. She landed. She pecked, scratched and - for good measure - reverted to the tried and tested shit spreading technique.

First, there was shrieking. Arms flapped, body parts flapped, and Henrietta fled. The only thing in her favour was Dan's lack of enthusiasm for going outside in a state of undress; she had as long as it took him to put on pants and a t-shirt in which to escape. She got to the front door just as he started to half run, half fall down the stairs. She got though the flap just as he made a wild swipe for her trailing left leg. The door was locked, which gave her a five second head start as he fumbled with the lock and scanned the garden for her retreating tail feathers. He spotted her as she darted through the hedge; a manoeuvre that he was rather oversized for. That gave her a little more time.

Why did the chicken cross the road? In order to escape from a teenager in his pants, obviously.

On the other side of the road, a tiny gap under a fence was just enough for Henrietta to get through, into someone else's garden and a freedom that she was in no way ready for. As she roosted in a bush at the end of a stranger's lawn that evening, she found herself running through the same questions over and over again:

1. Do I have food?

2. Is there a fox?

3. Where are my eggs?

4. Is it raining?

5. Can I smell 'cat'?

6. Is that a fox?

7. Do I have food?

8. Why can I see green eyes glowing on the ground?

9. How do I get up there?

10. Why does my bum[35] hurt?

11. Can I eat this?

12. What's that noise?

13. Does that smell like a fox?

14. Why is that bird attacking me?

15. Is that a worm?

16. Is that fluffy thing a cat?

Other beings with a better tuned chicken brain would have been better at answering these questions. It particular, they

---

[35] Chickens don't have bums, they have cloacas. Did we establish whether it was cloaci or cloacas?? Most chickens don't know this though, because they're chickens. They certainly don't know the etymology of 'cloaca' nor indeed the concept of etymology.

might have spotted that, yes. That fluffy thing is definitely a cat.

Idris

Idris was an egg, but only briefly. In a heartbeat he was surrounded by a cacophony of chirruping and was quickly aware that something was standing on his head. It's possible that it was even jumping on his head. He was tiny and confused and his legs didn't even work properly. After several failed attempts, he got himself upright and started a lifelong obsession with food.

Idris emerged from his eggy prison into a new prison, which was a shed full of shelves. Every shelf had a billion other chickens on it and they all seemed to hate him. In fact, they all seemed to have a mutual hatred of every other component of chickenhood in the universe; there was a general aura of 'angry' in the room.

Moving around wasn't really an option; he couldn't even see the floor, or his own little feet. Every morning[36], someone opened a door, blinded a billion chickens and threw some seeds in their general direction. They fought over the seeds, then they fought over the floor and at times they seemed to be fighting over the air itself. This was not a safe environment for a child, so it was a good job that social services didn't stretch to the chicken world.

Occasionally, some of his compadres were taken out and never came back. It was a blessing because it meant that for a short time there was space to dance and space to breathe. Sadly, there was then an ensuing crush towards the void, which ironically voided the void.

---

[36] It may or may not have been morning. It was completely dark in there and there was no window onto the outside world

After an eternity[37] of squabbling over unidentified seeds, attacking anything that dared to stand on his feet and repeatedly learning that chickens really can't fly, it was Idris' turn to leave.

The bright lights of the outside were a lot to take in and Idris shut his eyes. He had no idea how long for or what the world on the other side of his eyelids looked like, but as his eyes fluttered open, his world was turned upside-down. Not metaphorically, but actually. He was dangling upside down in a cage with his feet tied together. Both parts of his brain were clear that this was bad news.

There were lots of loud voices, generally repeating the same things over and over again, but Idris couldn't work out what they were, largely because his vocabulary didn't stretch far beyond "Cluck?" or possible - on a good day - "CLUCK!". There was a lull in the shouting and a new person nearby.

There was the chink of coin against coin, and a quieter conversation.

Then there was a hand in the cage, and Idris was unceremoniously wrenched back out into the sunlight. He pecked at the hand holding him for a bit, but stopped when it swung him around like a helicopter and shouted something unintelligible[38] at him. Gravity was sending all of his blood in the wrong direction, because apparently Idris was - again - upside down. Had he known what the world looked like, he would have realised that everything was the wrong way up. Just as he was starting to feel dizzy, Idris

---

[37] Eight weeks is perhaps more of an eternity for a chicken than for a person.

[38] Of course it was unintelligible. He was a chicken.

was laid down on a flat surface in a darker place. Next to him, a flat shiny thing glinted in the sunlight that pierced the tiny window above him. Those of us who have watched crime thrillers on TV will know that a flat shiny thing in the vicinity of a trussed up body is generally bad news. Idris, on the other hand, just thought it was pretty.

Idris stood up. Except of course he didn't stand up, because his feet were tied together. What actually happened was a comedy wiggle, followed by some ineffectual flapping, and a reduction in the size of the gap between Idris and the edge of the worktop. Idris was not aware of the concept of gravity and therefore had absolutely no idea of his impending peril; neither from the flat shiny thing, nor from a collision with the floor.

He watched as the owner of the flat shiny thing came over and picked it up. He watched as it went up and down, casting odd reflections around the room. He watched as a white spherical thing became a small heap of tiny cubes, as the flat shiny thing whirred up and down like a machine. He cried. This was not an emotional response to the destruction before his eyes - it was a physiological response to a dismembered onion.

He watched as the flat shiny thing went back into action over a pointy orange thing. He watched as the pointy orange thing was turned to debris. Idris was never going to have an IQ far above 12, but he was starting to get the impression that the flat shiny thing was working its way in his general direction. Having seen what it did to the other ingredients of the meal with Idris at its heart, he decided that he needed to be somewhere else as a matter of some urgency.

Moments later, Idris was saved by a bell. Literally a bell. It was attached to something with four furry legs that said "Miaow?" when it saw Idris. It jumped up onto the worktop next to him and gave him a sniff. It had bad breath. It had sharp claws. It gave an 'I'm really hungry' vibe. It drew back one paw, and Idris tensed every muscle in his body, ready to escape[39]. Just as the furry thing looked set to end Idris' short life, a person scooped him up and took him away. Idris seized his chance and started what was perhaps the slowest and most ridiculous escape in the history of chickenhood.

He flapped and wriggled, flapped and wriggled and then wriggled and flapped. The edge of the worktop loomed, and then so did the floor, swiftly afterwards. He flapped frantically as the floor got closer to his face, slowing his descent like a really badly designed parachute. He hit the ground with more of a 'splat' than a thump, thus completing Escape Plan Part One.

Escape Plan Part Two consisted of: Think really quickly because you don't have a bloody clue what you're doing next.

Idris dug his beak into the wooden floor and dragged himself a few centimetres across the floor. Then a few more. Then his face started to hurt so he tried getting some traction with his feet instead. That was a much noisier system but it did seem to be more efficient and it was certainly less painful. Idris was incredibly lucky that the

---

[39] To confirm, Idris was really stupid. **Really** stupid. He had already forgotten that he was trussed up like… well… like a chicken. He wasn't escaping anywhere in a hurry. Or at all, really.

owner of the house was a four-legged fluffy[40] fan and this particular cat was incredibly lucky that there were fish entrails on offer. These two facts combined to make the perfect storm for a chicken escaping in high definition slow motion.

After about five minutes, Idris had covered about a metre of ground in the kitchen. He had no idea where he was going or even where he was, but he was heading towards what he would eventually find out was the toilet. The wriggling and scrabbling of feet was phrenetic and uncoordinated, and eventually it did some serious damage to the string that was tying his feet together. All of the chicken gods[41] were aligned and Idris broke free. His weak little legs sprung into action and he waddled unsteadily in the direction of a dark room that he hoped would not have a flat shiny thing (or a cat) in it.

Just as he skidded around the corner into that dark room, the owner of the house ran out of patience with the 'playful' cat which had by now drawn blood. She was all set to remove Idris' head with her flat, shiny friend, but there was no chicken there to decapitate. She stared at the space where she was certain she had left it and ran through several scenarios in her head. She took a step back for a wider angle of the scene. This put her left foot directly on top of the incriminating string that had bound Idris. It stuck to the mud on her shoe, and travelled back to the market

---

[40] Idris had absolutely no idea what a cat was, or how to recognise one. You and I, with our combined IQs of considerably more than 12, know that it was a cat. For the sake of clarity, let's just call it a cat.

[41] I am not convinced they are a plural entity.

with her when she went back to buy a chicken to replace the chicken she wasn't sure she hadn't bought.

The toilet was a vile corner of the house - not connected to any sewage system and basically just a bucket with an ill-fitting lid. There were lots of flies and insufficient windows. Idris had spent a big chunk of his life surrounded by several inches of chicken shit and this was definitely worse. The tiny remnants of human brain residing in his skull suggested that he should check his route before running blindly into the kitchen. This served him well; the cat was back and the scraps of fish had not been enough to take that glint out of its eye. It didn't see Idris straight away though, which give him a tiny head start and a second to engage both of his brain cells at once. This swift action saved his life, because he stuck his head back into the fetid toilet[42] and waited. Above his head, a tiny window seemed the only alternative.

As we have established, chickens are largely flightless. However, it's extraordinary what the body can do under duress, and this was definitely what one might call duress. The 'ess' suffix almost implies something small or feminine or cute, which is the exact opposite of the real meaning of the word. There was nothing small, feminine or cute about being chased by felicidal[43] cat into a room full of shit.

Idris took a deep breath and jumped towards the light of the small open window. He got about 30cm above the ground, which was nowhere near high enough. The noise of his inelegant landing alerted his pursuer to his location. He tried again. He got a little bit higher but still fell a long way short

---

[42] 'Toilet' here refers to the room, not the bucket.

[43] I have absolutely made this word up. It's the cat version of 'homicide', which you probably worked out.

of his intended destination. He landed again, at exactly the same time as the cat came through the door. When I say 'exactly', I really do mean exactly. Idris' feet planted themselves firmly in the cat's face, which was as much of a surprise to the cat as it was to Idris. The cat leapt off the ground like it had landed on a hot tin roof, and this was like a springboard for Idris, giving him the height he needed to throw himself towards the window. He flapped his pointless wings enough to get him onto the edge of the open window and then out into freedom. 'Freedom', for Idris, was a busy main road.

Crossing the road is not a skill that comes naturally to many animals - even those much brighter than Idris. Something vaguely human told him that these big metal boxes weren't going to do him any favours. They were bigger and faster than him, and each individual tyre probably had more intellectual capacity than an entire flock of chickens. In a stroke of something nestled between 'brave' and 'stupid', he made a run for it. Like a 1980s computer game, he stepped nimbly from space to space between the speeding cars and - with the chicken gods once again smiling down on him - got safely to the other side[44].

On the other side of the road, Idris could see between the other buildings and into the wilderness beyond. He had absolutely no idea what he was seeing, but he liked the look of it and didn't have any better ideas. He scuttled off into the undergrowth, which felt like exactly where he was meant to be. He danced through the leaves and branches on the floor, loving the feeling on his feet and the wind in his feathers. He leapt into the lower branches of a small tree, and stopped for a minute. He listened to all of the new

---

[44] There's a joke in there somewhere.

sounds around him. Whilst he didn't have the words for the things he was hearing, the other birds, the rustling, the cars on the road, children shouting, everything gave him joy. Most of it meant absolutely nothing to him, but there was one noise that stirred something in him.

"Cluck?"

It came from the ground beneath him and he was so excited that he shat on it. Even in chicken circles, this does not constitute a good first date. The beautiful creature below him made an angry noise[45], kicked some dirt around with its feet, and strutted off. From this point on, Idris was on some kind of autopilot and followed the love of his life through the brush. If it had been a cartoon, there would have been giant red hearts radiating from his eyes and his tongue would have been hanging out.

He saw a bug. He instinctively picked it up in his beak and scuttled in front of her to make his offering. He dropped it in front of her like the chicken equivalent of a bunch of flowers, and stepped back to admire his gesture. His gesture flipped itself over and ran away. This did not bode well. So far he had shat on her and given her an escaping gift. 'Romance' doesn't count for much in the average chicken psyche, but things were clearly awry here.

The tiny 'human' part of his brain gushed briefly. If it had been bigger, it might have come out with something like: "I've seen you strutting around here and you look like the

---

[45] Probably?

most beautiful chick[46] I have ever set my beady[47] eyes on and I'd love to get to know you better. Can I take you for some ants and a dust bath? I know some excellent places…"

Of course, given his species, what he actually said was "Cluck", and then put his head on one side in a way that he (and she) may or may not have thought was coy.

The female chicken (we'll call her Sarah, for no particular reason) stared at him. He had absolutely no idea what this meant or what to do next, but fortunately chickens don't need to know what to do next. He didn't need to work through the concept of consent or contraception or come up with chat-up lines that showed his beautiful spouse what he thought of her. He stepped wobblingly[48] towards her and the rest seems to have happened on auto-pilot.

If you are faint-hearted, you might want to skip this next paragraph; it may fill in some gaps in your knowledge of the animal kingdom which you would perhaps prefer remained unfilled.

Idris trotted behind Sarah, jumped and flapped a bit, and her red cloaca popped into view. This was all he needed and enough to inspire his next move. He flapped and

---

[46] Normally, the term 'chick' is condescending and a perfect example of everyday sexism. In this context it was totally accurate.

[47] Have you ever looked a chicken in the eye(s)? No. Of course you haven't. Why would you. Anyway - they really do have beady eyes. Eyes like beads. Staring, unfeeling and really quite disturbing if you stare at them for long enough, although frankly I have no idea why you would.

[48] Yes. This is another made up word.

jumped (flumped) behind her until he mounted her. If there is a god, he must have been drinking when he created chicken anatomy because it is frankly ridiculous. Female chickens have an orifice and male chickens have an orifice. They have to rub together and the male chicken squirts his romantic juices in the general direction of the female orifice, and then that's that. This, therefore, is exactly what Idris did. He rubbed and squelched at Sarah and then dismounted, in a courtship that lasted less than 60 seconds. He felt the need to rearrange his feathers, then he pecked about in the dirt for a bit.

In that brief moment, Idris ensured the survival of his bloodline. There was a tiny hint of pride somewhere in his tiny brain and he felt the need to stay near Sarah, although he had no idea why. Half an hour later, he found himself gathering twigs and bits of dry grass, which he heaped up under a bush. Instinctively, he and Sarah then began weaving them all together into a messy masterpiece exactly the same size as Sarah. That evening, they roosted together. Sarah in her nest and Idris in the tree above on lookout[49]. When a stray dog came close to his beloved, Idris threw his whole body at its' face, wheeling about like an angry windmill on speed. The dog could have literally eaten Idris alive but was perturbed by his confident assault, and instead ran away.

Had the dog been a person, it would probably have told his children not to go anywhere near the mad bastard in the tree.

---

[49] This is new territory. This is not what chickens do in the wild, mainly because chickens are far too stupid to survive in the wild. Idris had the advantage here, in the form of the inexplicable remnants of humanness that hid somewhere in the depths of his brain.

Idris kept up sentry duty for ten days. He gathered seeds and insects for Sarah and he rarely left her side. When other species appeared anywhere near her, he found inner reserves of anger and strength that gave Sarah the same level of protection as a pack of wolves with an entourage of geese and hippos.

After ten days, she grunted in a way that he hadn't heard her grunt before. She looked uncomfortable for a bit. Then, with minimal fuss, she laid an egg.

The next 20 days was excruciatingly dull for all concerned. Sarah sat in her nest and occasionally got up and wandered off. Idris gathered food and tried to look busy. He checked the nest at least a million times a second and danced around like a lizard on really hot sand. Nothing else happened at all; clearly all of the other creatures within a ten mile radius had got the memo that Idris a chicken possessed, and he was not to be messed with.

On day 21, he heard the most beautiful noise he had ever heard. A feeble 'tap' from somewhere inside the precious shell. Then another. Then two together, and a rest. Sarah was still sitting on her egg, but when it started moving independently, she shot out of the nest and squawked.

The egg wobbled.

It cracked.

It went frighteningly quiet.

The crack widened.

The whole shell was bisected and a tiny (and incredibly ugly) head popped out. Parents always love their babies but to everyone else they always look pretty rough. This bald monstrosity was no exception, with bulgy eyes, impossibly small wings and wrinkled skin that was almost see-through.

The weirdly wonderful thing about the horrific creature before them, was that Sarah and Idris could see a tiny heart beating under that paper-thin bag of skin. It was the most beautiful thing they had ever seen.

Somewhere high up above them, something briefly cast a shadow over their fledgling[50] family, and was gone.

Claudia (the chick, obviously) learned to walk a few hours later, and things were looking peachy.

Until they weren't.

A few hours after parenthood arrived in Idris' life, he learned to fly. For the shortest of moments he thought it was some kind of miracle, and he flapped his wings enthusiastically. His bliss was short-lived though, as the talons in his shoulders tightened and the ground slipped away beneath him. The eagle into whose stomach he would shortly be travelling had not received the memo about Idris' ferocity, and now he was on the wrong side of gravity. It was Game Over for Idris.

---

[50] Fledgling. Did you see what I did there?

Claudia

Claudia had inherited all of her father's human brain, but she shirked even more known science than he had, and her human brain grew at the same rate as she did. At one week old, she had twice the speed of Sarah (which wasn't hard) and infinitely more grey matter. Her relative genius meant that her head was totally out of proportion and she was hilariously top-heavy. It meant that when she ran, the weight of her head pressed her forward and her knobbly little legs had to sprint to keep up. The result was like a perpetual motion machine of some kind; always in a state of flux and somewhere between sprinting and face-planting.

She knew that this was not a place where she was safe. She knew that her mum was in 'chocolate teapot' territory as far as protecting her was concerned, and she knew that she needed to - metaphorically - fly away. This was a confused chicken in need of a plan.

The plan came unexpectedly, in the form of a child on a bike.

The bike had a basket on the front, with what was probably a school bag in it. The school bag was roughly the same size as a small chicken, which was fortunate for Claudia, as she was coincidentally the same size as a school bag.

It turned out that the child was not an animal lover. This became clear when the child ran after Sarah with a stick, screaming "Die chicken, die". Claudia felt this was incontrovertible evidence that the child was more of an animal that Claudia herself. Her mother's suffering was a helpful distraction and it gave her enough time to half climb, half jump and half fly[51] into the basket and dive into the bag. Opening the bag would have made this endeavour simpler but she rectified this tiny oversight and took a second attempt at diving. Inside the bag was a sandwich, and life took a turn for the better.

Claudia felt that she should avenge her mother, so she shat in the school bag and squelched it around amongst the general bag debris. This made her feel smug and superior, neither of which are normal emotions for chickens.

There was a squawk, then there was a scream. The scream contained words that Claudia suspected were perhaps inappropriate for a child, but she had no idea what those words were. She was, after all, a chicken. Shortly after that, the child came back and the bag (and its chicken passenger) juddered off through undergrowth and back onto solid ground. Our plucky little friend discovered that she suffered from travel sickness, and quickly refunded the sandwich.

When the bike stopped, the bag was grabbed and thrown into a dark place. Claudia dragged herself out and began picking bits of part-digested sandwich out of her still-fluffy feathers. She made a nest in a wellington boot and sock combo, and went to sleep. At the time, this seemed like a great idea but she hadn't entirely thought the concept through. You see, dear reader, wellington boots are designed to have feet in them, not baby chickens. She was therefore rudely awakened by the sight of an unsocked and slightly crusty looking foot moving rapidly towards her. The only thing working in her favour was her beak.

---

[51] This is figurative. I am aware that this is not how halves work.

Tilting her head back weaponised her face and the crusty foot was impaled. The owner of the foot made a noise very similar to the one her mum had made the day before and then withdrew, throwing the wellington boot to the ground and stomping off. Claudia scuttled out and found herself in the hallway of a house.

When she was sure there was nobody else nearby, she went to explore. Stairs were a problem; there was nothing to get a grip on and she simply couldn't jump high enough. Back down the hallway and into the kitchen, she found a tiled floor as shiny as ice and unscalable walls. She also found crumbs and she liked the crumbs a lot. In the corner of the room she found sticks with colourful ends and flat white stuff which she had an urge to play with.

The sticks nestled neatly between her toes and left a very satisfying mark on the flat white stuff. After chasing the flat sticks around on the floor for a bit, she realised she had created a sequence of squiggles and shapes that formed a pattern of some kind. When she stepped back and looked at them, her messed up brain knew that they were letters, and that the letters spelled out

H E L P M F

The 'F' seemed wrong but the rest resonated. She left them in the middle of the floor and hid in a plant pot. She felt like she was finally in control of her young life, as she sat back and watched chaos unfold.

An adult came into the room and saw the note. The adult burst into tears and ran out again, returning with another adult who responded in exactly the same way. 'Confused' would be an inadequate term for whatever emotion it was that was blindsiding Claudia. Why weren't they immediately concerned for her wellbeing? Why hadn't they called an animal charity or something? Shouldn't they have been making her a safe nest to curl up in?

There was a conversation, then one of the adults left the room and came back with a smaller person wearing a single wellington boot. The smaller person was put gently down on a chair, and both adults crouched down to have an earnest conversation, which Claudia was only privy to pockets of.

"…you said that…"

"…yes… no… I didn't…"

"…write that…?"

"…wasn't… foot…" <tears>

"WHAT?"

"…I didn't write anything!"

Then there were cuddles and more tears and silence.

Claudia watched as the two adults embraced and trailed snot on each others' shoulders. She listened as they discussed whether their child was experiencing significant trauma that they weren't aware of. There was a brief accusation of unfunny pranking made by one, followed by some words that would have made Claudia blush if a) it was possible for chickens to blush and b) she knew what they meant.

All in all, Escape Plan #1 was an unmitigated failure, which opened up a whole new dilemma in her otherwise uncomplicated life. Should she try and fix the issues she had created for this little family, or should she high-tail it out of there and out into the world. In the short term, she was warm and comfortable in the plant pot; the decision was taken out of her hands because she fell asleep.

It was the screaming that woke her. Or was it the barking. No wait… Maybe it was the beeping. The cacophony which bounced around inside her tiny skull made her eyes hurt. Peeking out from her planter, she could see a dog with its back legs taped together and red paint on its paws, leaving a trail of paw prints across far too much of the kitchen floor.

The plant that Claudia was nesting in was a well established rubber plant with a coir support running up through the middle that she could easily scale. From the top she had a better view of the chaos. If she'd had the appropriate vocal equipment, she would have laughed out loud… There was smoke coming from the corner of the kitchen, and one adult was flapping an oven tray around to dissipate the smoke. From the depths of the fog came another adult, with a small child under one arm and a towel in the other. It was trying to herd the dog, presumably in order to de-paint it. The dog was extraordinarily adept at avoiding capture, considering its tape-based woes, and the adult was significantly impeded by the feral child under its arm. Given the amount of flailing, it was a miracle that nobody was airborne.

The flapping adult lost grip on the oven tray, which flew across the room and knocked an open bottle of milk onto the floor. The dog skidded through the milk, its paws scrabbling frantically through the puddle but getting nowhere. The puddle of milk started turning pink from the paint, which made the kitchen look like a murder scene. The dog stood on the oven tray and skidded across the room as though it was in training for the Winter Olympics, and came to a halt with its nose directly in line with Claudia's beak. She very gently poked him with her pointy face and that tipped him over the edge.

Chickens tend not to have an excellent concept of time[52] so we will stick with the frustratingly vague 'some time passed'. In that unspecified period of time, Claudia learned a lot of swear words, saw a complete canine breakdown, and discovered that - although children can't smash glass with their screaming - they are prepared to try really hard.

There was paint and clothing and milk and fur everywhere. Whatever had been in the oven was definitely a new carbon-based lifeform. The child had apparently run out of air and was quiet. The adults had run out of marbles and wore a face that said 'despair'. Claudia was still stuck in her plant pot and it was starting to get dark. Just at the point when the whole situation couldn't possibly have got more 'cartoon' if it tried, it got more cartoon. A cat emerged through what turned out to be a cat-flap in the back door. It surveyed the room with disdain and then went to work cleaning up the milk. The dog whimpered. The adults collectively sighed. Then the cat's nose twitched.

The little pink nose moved almost imperceptibly, then it looked up. If it's possible for a cat to raise an eyebrow, then that's what the cat did. It sniffed. It stiffened. Then it very slowly started making its way across the room to the plant pot where an increasingly frightened small fluffy bird was stationed. Claudia did not have a contingency plan for a cat attack, and did not have long to formulate one. The cat

---

[52] Where would they put a wristwatch? It would be highly impractical around an ankle… They'd fall over every time they did a time check.

knew it was winning, and it gained what could only be described as a swagger as it trotted towards its dinner.

Using every single remnant of grey matter, Claudia raced through a million scenarios of what might happen next[53] and tried to find an exit strategy. She couldn't.

As she made her peace with god and the cat's stomach juices started to flow, the universe leapt to the little chick's aid in the form of a recently awake small child with limited regard for animal rights. The child ambled sleepily into the milky room, saw the cat and launched a lego bomb in the cat's general direction. The shrapnel exploded across the floor and the cat mad a vertical leap then skidded back outside on feet that didn't appear to touch the ground. Claudia had her reprieve and as the last rays of the sun disappeared, the frazzled household made its way to bed.

Leaving the house before morning seemed like an excellent priority, and our plucky little clucker began her reconnaissance immediately. On the other side of the kitchen was the hallway she had originally come from, and beyond that there was a door. In the door there was a letterbox and Claudia had an inkling that it would take her outside, if only she could reach it. She just needed to be 90cm taller.

With the strength of a scaled-up ant, she dragged a cornflake box, an empty shoebox, a board game and two trainers into a heap that got her up to 84cm, and she decided that she could jump the rest. She bounced until she could force her beak into the flap of the letter box, and then

---

[53] Actually there was just one, which revolved around her untimely death, Every avenue of thought she attempted ended up in her demise.

scrabbled her feet and flapped her pointless wings until she was somewhere in the middle of the door. Forcing her way out of the opposite flap, she plopped to the ground with a sigh of relief, and scuttled off into a bush. No doubt the family blamed their child for the random pile of stuff in front of the door, and no doubt the child was very upset by this. Claudia, however, did not give a shit.

In the front garden there was an assortment of hideous gnomes and accessories. One of the gnomes was standing outside a badly proportioned house, brandishing a giant spade. This offered Claudia an excellent place to hide; it was dry, dark and hidden in plain sight. The entrance was also far too small for a cat, which was excellent news. She dragged in some dry leaves and as many twigs as she could be bothered to gather, then curled up and went to sleep in a gnome's living room. Over the following few weeks, she learned to dig for worms and occasionally found berries and other delectables that had fallen from bushes in the front garden. When she was feeling brave, she shot out to a vantage point at the base of the fence, and watched what went on below. She learned which cars lived nearby, which children went this way to school, who the post was delivered by and who often dropped crumbs of their breakfast en route to work. As a byproduct of this latter fact, she also learned that croissants were way better than worms.

Eventually, there came a sad moment when Claudia realised that she had outgrown the gnome's house, and would need somewhere else to live. She had developed a fairly comprehensive understanding of the local area and learned quite a lot about the personalities of the native population. She knew which dogs were cute and cuddly, and which were vicious beasts. She knew what order people walked past and she knew which of them were generally nice humans. One in particular was a cautious older lady who rode a bike very slowly on the pavement every morning. Claudia had no idea where she was going, but had seen her stop to help a lost child and that seemed like a good sign. After positioning herself between the bars of the fence in readiness, our heroine dropped soundlessly into the wicker basket on the front of the lady's bike and away to freedom.

That does, of course, depend on your definition of 'freedom'.

Claudia jiggled about in the basket for a while, until the bike stopped and its owner dismounted. Claudia was still small enough to hitch a ride on the back of her rucksack and took her chances as the lady walked over the threshold and into what Claudia hoped would be her new home. As the front door closed behind her, she descended into her very own personal hell.

On the floor below her, the unmistakable sound of her nemesises[54] rang out.

"Miaow"

"MEEEAOW"

"ReeeeAAgh"

"PrrrrrrrrrrRRrrrrrrrrrrr"

"...eaow?"

---

[54] It sounds quite Latin so I would hazard a guess that the plural of 'nemesis' is 'nemeses' and not nemesises. The trouble is, I don't care enough to check.

<hiss>

“Meeeeeeeeaaaaaaaaaaaoooow?”

“Mew”

Some of them seemed to be shouting, some of them seemed to be quite friendly. At least one was angry. All were unmistakably hungry, and Claudia was unmistakably edible.

The lady went through to the kitchen and her feline clan swelled as she got closer to the place where the food was presumably kept. She greeted them all by name, stood on two, screeched when one tried to climb up her leg, and bent to rub a couple of the friendlier ones. Claudia held on for dear life, and was relieved when the horde of cats were sidetracked by several tonnes of biscuits that were liberally thrown in the general direction of an assortment of bowls on the floor. The lady and her hitcher went upstairs and Claudia once again got a brief reprieve. This was not the safe-haven she had hoped for; it was actually the lethal lair of a crazy cat lady with more cats than a partially human chicken was capable of counting.

She needed to escape. Again.

She measured her time in cat biscuits, and it equated to ‘not very long’.

The older lady had gone upstairs with one fairly small cat clinging onto her cardigan. Claudia felt that one small cat gave her better odds that what seemed like twelve billion cats in the kitchen. They seemed to be in a bedroom, which was a good reason for Claudia to be in any room that **wasn’t** that bedroom. She flapped/climbed out and into another room, then up some curtains so she could perch on a bookcase. She hid between "101 chicken recipes" and "Taxidermy for beginners"[55].

Apparently this particular older lady really felt the cold because the temperature in the room climbed to 'oven' level, which sent Claudia into a sleepy torpor for an unspecified length of time. When she woke up, it was dark in the room, apart from the two evil glowing orbs staring unflinchingly up at her from ground level.

"...eaow?"

The creature was clearly possessed because it didn't blink. It didn't move. It was like one of those reflective sculptures that people put in their gardens to scare animals away[56]. Claudia stared back, occasionally cocking her head on one side to remind the cat that she was real. She made a face which she thought made her look rough, tough and mean, forgetting that it was dark and she was chicken. No chicken in history has ever looked 'tough'.

The cat was unperturbed, and through some kind of gliding motion, it seemed to be getting closer. This made Claudia uncomfortable and she felt she needed to warn it off. She wriggled behind "101 chicken recipes" and put all of her weight behinds she could push it off the shelf into the area previously occupied by the cat. Cats are fast, and apparently vengeful. It reappeared, but with an added hint of growling. "Taxidermy for beginners" was next. The cat spun

---

[55] Claudia would have been concerned by this, had she been able to read. It was perhaps a blessing that she couldn't.

[56] I know cats are pretty dumb but are they really dumb enough to be fooled by an aluminium cut-out? Yes, they are.

expertly on its own axis and avoided the second missile. Several ornaments, some tinsel and one hairbrush later and the cat was enraged. This was not helping. What if it summoned its friends? There was nothing left to throw and no backup plan. Claudio's last remaining weapon was her beak. She adopted a 'divebomb' pose and jumped off the top shelf with what she hoped was both elegance and menace. The cat saw her coming and simply sidestepped, allowing Claudia to dive-bomb into the thick-pile carpet, where her beak got stuck. If cats could laugh, this one would be pissing itself.

Our plucky little clucker was baffled by what happened next. The cat put one paw (claws sheathed) on Claudia's back to hold her down, opened her mouth and bent down towards Claudia's face. While she silently clucked her goodbyes and made one last prayer to whoever her god was, the cat very gently loosened her beak from the carpet and then picked her up by the neck.

Any normal feline would dismember the chicken at this point, then lay out the bitter bits in places where nobody would see them until after they had stood on them. This was no normal feline. It took Claudia to the back door, pushed the cat flap open and carefully deposited her outside. The flap flapped shut, and a moist and confused fowl lay motionless on the mat, listening to the sounds of the night, competing in volume with her own heartbeat.

The 'sounds of the night' swiftly became the sounds of the rest of the cats in the house realising there was a gift on the doormat outside. Her fluffy friend defended the catfap vigorously while Claudia got her bearings and made a run for it. There was a pickup truck parked next door and its engine was running. She leapt into the back and closed her eyes.

For a couple of minutes, the pickup drove at a steady pace along a residential street. Claudia's feathers were ruffled but she was so relieved that she didn't care. As the driver picked up the pace a bit, she was knocked off her feet and had to grip the floor with her feet. When her feet started to slip too, she held on with her beak. At around 58mph she could hold on no longer. When driving at just under the national speed limit, chickens can fly. As the unsuspecting Volvo driver gasped and tried to swerve, the last thing Claudia heard was

"Fuuuuuuu…"

Ken

Ken woke up small. Something warm and pink was caressing him and it made him feel warm and fuzzy inside right up until the moment it said "Moo".

Ken was man enough to know what a cow was and chicken enough to want to run away. His ridiculous little legs made his escape a long and drawn-out affair; the neighbourly cow could easily follow him at a gentle stroll. Ken stopped on a mole-hill and gasped for breath, his little chest heaving at the effort of having run 20 metres as his first ever steps into life. He was only slightly bigger than a ping-pong ball and anything like a hiding place was an impossible distance away. Daisy[57] licked him again. The first time it had teased his lifeless body into the land of the living. The second time it was just gross. Ken made an angry-ish squeak and pecked at whatever parts of Daisy's legs she could reach, so Daisy scooped him up with her massive tongue and deftly sucked him into her mouth. She didn't grind and she didn't swallow but she felt that he should have been grateful for being licked to life, and did not appreciate his lack of thanks. She carried him to the edge of the field, deposited him on top of a dry stone wall, and walked away. She probably thought[58] that she was banishing him from the pleasure of her company, but in fact she was rescuing him.

The floor was a long way away. It didn't take a genius to work out that he needed to ground level, which was handy; Ken was no genius. He cowered for a minute, watching the

---

[57] Why are cows always called after grassy flowers? Daisy, Buttercup, Clover… Why not ragwort or corncockle…

[58] 'Thought' is a bit of an overstatement.

world around him. Magpies jumped out of trees and took flight. Robins stepped effortlessly into nothing and flapped gracefully into the treetops. Blackbirds tucked in their wings, dropped like stones and then swooped out along the ground until they landed in the undergrowth. His rudimentary grasp of the laws of physics did not stop him from believing that he too could defy gravity as he stepped off the wall and flapped his tiny wings.

On the plus side, at least he hit the ground feet first. Had it been a Hollywood movie, he would have done a commando-roll and assumed a combat position from behind a handy rock. Sadly, this was not Hollywood and there was neither style nor grace in anything about his largely vertical journey to the floor. He landed in an indeterminate mound of animal excrement and sunk in up to his chest. Several uncomfortable minutes of squelching later, he found himself back on solid ground and feeling (but not smelling) lucky. He shook some of the chunks off and took a step out towards his future.

Apparently, his 'future' was underground.

Our bird-brained hero took a single small step into a rabbit hole, then rolled until all sources of light and sense of direction were gone, then wobbled unsteadily in the first direction that took him. He could hear something in the distance but didn't have the IQ to realise that 'something' could be bad news.

The 'something' got closer. Ken carried on wobbling towards it until he walked straight into it and it was like colliding with a warm cloud. Nothing in Ken's tiny brain suggested that it might be something dangerous so Ken curled up and went to sleep.

There is very little difference between the intelligence of a rabbit and that of a chicken. The mummy rabbit that Ken had stumbled upon had no idea that Ken did not have big floppy ears and eat carrots because it was dark. The first big clue came when Ken tried to suckle; his beak was not conducive to a comfortable maternal moment and Rosie the Rabbit was less than impressed. In a typically rabbitty attack, she kicked him away to the other side of the 'room'. It was a short flight.

The stubborn remnants of human genetic dirt left somewhere in Ken's DNA pointed out to him that he was not a rabbit and therefore should probably not trust his 'rabbit' instincts. He also knew he wasn't a pigeon, which meant he had no homing instinct and no idea which way he needed to go down what was literally a rabbit's warren of tunnels. He waddled blindly in the darkness until he hit something and had to change direction. It wasn't a particularly scientific method but he kept doing it until he found a new tunnel and continued bouncing from side to earthy side until a fresh bundle of fluff came thundering towards him and knocked him sprawling. In the short term, he briefly became a misplaced rug but in the longer term it surely meant that the bundle of fluff must have come from somewhere, and Ken knew that he needed to be similarly somewhere. Off he went, like a bumper car being driven by a blind person, until he reached a junction. He opted for the tunnel that seemed have a suggestion of a breeze. His little legs pounded the soil until he eventually popped up in the middle of an entirely different field. Feeling a combination of proud, excited and shattered, he took a moment to rest.

The split second it took him to sit down was a split second too long; a colossal bird swooped down - apparently from nowhere - and took him in its talons. He flapped his wings pointlessly and then gave up and looked at the scenery. He was swiftly becoming the best-travelled chick in the country, but he had a sinking feeling that he would also be one of the shortest lived. He looked at the claws that held him prisoner, and the legs they were attached to. On a whim, he thrust his beak deep into one of them, and its owner instinctively let go.

Win!

He did the same thing to the other leg and very briefly celebrated his success. His celebrations were cut short by a rediscovery of gravity...

The tiny houses and trees got gradually less tiny until it dawned on Ken that he was going to land on one of them. He was no structural engineer, but Ken was fairly certain that 'tree' would be a softer landing than 'house'. Ken stuck out his ridiculous wings and used them like a wing suit to aim towards what looked like the bushiest vegetation available. On closer inspection he was clearly wrong, but by then it was too late to do anything about it. He hit one hard, thorny branch, followed by a succession of similarly thorny branches until he was perforated like a colander. The tree definitely broke his fall, along with several of his bones. Ironically, by the time he'd been tickled by every nasty branch on an aggressive hawthorn tree, he actually hit the ground quite gently.

His recent brush with death made Ken want to crawl into a hole and hide for an indeterminate length of time. He would have licked his wounds if it was an option.

As we have already discovered, chickens can suffer from concussion and being beaten up by a tree is an incredibly good way to guarantee concussion. When Ken came around he knew nothing. He didn't know where he was or what he was doing. In fact, he didn't even really know that he was a chicken, or that he was inside a tree.

Strangely[59], the human bits of him started to ooze out at this point. He stood up and felt like he needed a calming drink[60] and a comfortable bed. Unsteady on his feet, he tottered towards one of the buildings that he'd had the foresight to avoid landing on and walked right through the front door. In the living room there was a group of people having a very civilised chat over tea. Ken boldly walked up to the foot of the sofa, started a 'conversation' with the closest human, and then hopped on up to sit beside him. He helped himself to a beak full of lukewarm tea, then snuggled up to his new best friend and went back to sleep.

The REAL humans in the room were speechless; he was behaving exactly like a 7cm fluffy human with a beak. The man he snuggled up next to felt guilty disturbing him (and had also gone off his tea). His friends had no context for a situation like this and there was a long pause while they processed the situation; nobody quite had the words for "there's a chicken on the sofa", so they defaulted to talking about the weather and managed to largely forget about the interloper, until he yawned and stretched his wings. What do humans very often want after a good sleep? A shower. Obviously.

Ken fought his way up every one of the 18 steps to the bathroom, jumped onto the handle of the shower to turn it on, and jumped down into the bathtub to enjoy his shower.

---

[59] Because this story isn't strange enough already...

[60] Probably tea, because that is the answer to everything.

The assembled company had followed him upstairs and felt weirdly uncomfortable watching him in the shower, but it was a good job they did; the shower was wonderfully powerful for a human but dangerously overpowered for a chicken. He was swept abruptly towards the plughole, where his fluffiness plugged the plughole and the water level in the bath started to rise. Before he drowned, his new favourite human scooped him up, wrapped him in a towel and rubbed him dry. This was strangely soothing and soporific - Ken's little head started nodding and putting him to bed seemed the most sensible thing to do[61]. The human tucked a sleepy Ken into the massive spare bed, tiptoed out and turned off the light.

He (we'll call him Malcolm. Why not?) stepped out onto the landing, and gestured "Sssssh" to his friends, then quickly realised that was absurd... but he still spoke in hushed tones as he crept downstairs to carry on his evening.

The next day, Malcolm felt like he'd adopted a child, when in fact he'd discovered a chicken. On autopilot, he made two cups of coffee and two pieces of toast with marmalade, and took them upstairs to the spare room. The door squeaked when he opened it, and Ken opened his eyes, his concussed little brain working overtime. Malcolm sat down next to him and started chattering about his plans for the day, then presented him with the toast. Ken was incredibly hungry and dived straight in there, feeling like the toast was no match for him. It was though, and after five minutes he'd gorged himself on as much toast as any baby chicken could possibly squeeze in, which equated to the size of a postage

---

[61] Let's have some clarity here. This really is a story about a chicken who thinks he's a person, being put to bed by a person who sees him as a human. Get over it; nobody said it was a documentary.

stamp. He tried coffee and decided he didn't like it, but the caffeine affected him instantly. He felt a splurge of energy surge through him and jumped out of bed to discuss his exciting plans for the day.

Whatever Malcolm said may as well have been Swahili to Ken and whatever Ken said might as well have been Hebrew to Malcolm; they were literally different species. They were both so wrapped up in their own worlds that neither was really listening to the other but they both babbled on regardless. Eventually, Malcolm stood up and expected Ken to do the same, but of course Ken was a chicken, so his 'standing up' apparatus was very different. This was the first moment in the whole bizarre morning when Malcolm rejoined the real world and recognised that this wasn't a normal relationship by any stretch of the imagination. He leaned forwards towards Ken and offered him the top pocket of his shirt. Ken jumped in, rearranged himself, and poked his head out so that he could see where he was going. Together, they went in to The Office.

Malcolm was an accountant for a small firm with a third floor office on the edge of town. When he walked into the office, all five of his colleagues stared at him and his new assistant. Oblivious, he sat down and opened his laptop to read the morning's emails. He occasionally said something to Ken, but was ostensibly talking to himself. At some point before lunch, Malcolm suddenly looked uncomfortable, and a damp patch slowly appeared around his pocket. Chickens poo. Chickens in pockets poo. Chickens in pockets who think they're people also poo. Pockets are not waterproof. If you put all of those facts together[62], you'll work out that Malcolm had a pocket full of shit. At this point, Malcolm

---

[62] ...and you're not a moron...

took a moment to evaluate his life choices, took Ken out of his pocket and changed into his gym kit.

Every now and then, Malcolm absent mindedly asked Ken to pass him something, and Ken obliged. While Malcolm didn't really think anything of it, to the assembled company it looked like the cleverest chicken in the world was working in their office.

This continued for several weeks until Ken was fully grown. Whilst his colleagues were impressed by Ken's manual and mental dexterity, they were also struggling with the fact that Malcolm seemed to be losing the plot and there was a chicken in the office. It was a well dressed chicken (Malcolm had gone to the trouble of making him a shirt and tie) and a well behaved chicken (Ken had started taking himself to the toilet), but the fact remained that Ken was still a chicken. They made a very peculiar pair, and drew a bit of a crowd wherever they went; there was never a dearth of people wanting to gawp at a well dressed chicken.

One evening, Malcom popped into a supermarket on his way home from work to buy some bread. With Ken on his shoulder, he chose a baguette and headed for the tills. As he turned the corner at the end of an aisle, his errant baguette hit an innocent shopper. It knocked some of the shopping out of her (very full) basket but Ken diligently hopped down to help her corral it back into the basket. She watched in awe, and then looked up at Malcolm, who was smiling at her. Basically:

Boy chooses baguette.

Baguette hits girl.

Girl meets chicken.

Girl falls in love with chicken.

Girl meets boy.

Girl realises boy makes better conversation than chicken.

Girl falls in love with boy.

Boy is largely oblivious to the whole process but eventually notices that the girl is holding his hand. Boy realises this is a good thing.

Just like the movies.

The 'girl' was called Lucy, and she quickly became a fixture in Malcolm's life. As is often the case, Malcolm threw everything into this new relationship and forgot about all of the things that already filled up his life. He had less and less time for Ken, whose concussion was fading and who was beginning to remember that he was in fact not a person. He had been with Malcom for the entirety of his conscious life and didn't know any other way to be, so Malcom's new-found romance was confusing and troublesome for Ken.

One miserable, moist and murky evening, Ken found himself watching a nature documentary on TV. Once, that would have been something that he did with Malcolm, but Malcolm was at a ballroom dancing lesson with Lucy. About half way through the programme, there was a scene where an eagle took a smaller bird from the ground in a silent attack. The eagle took its prey to its nest and carefully tore off strips for its brood of egrets. Somehow Ken thought "awwwww" and "arghghgh" at the same time. At the point where there were only feathers left anywhere near the nest, Ken realised that he was that small bird. He was the prey. He was the one who would be reduced to feathers if he got onto the wrong side of something with bigger claws than his. Without Malcom, he knew he was vulnerable to anything with teeth.

Ken had to leave.

If he was a person, he would have packed his bags and strutted out, slamming the door. He would have torn up some of Malcolm's shirts or written a letter full of 'truths' or maybe just shouted a lot.

But of course he wasn't a person. He was a chicken. His actual departure was considerably less dignified.

He scrabbled through a cat flap, shat himself, and caught three tail feathers in his own feet. He waddled to the end of the garden path and out into the fields beyond, feeling free and unburdened. The wind in his feathers, the clouds occasionally clearing the moon and the rain sploshing into little puddles on every hard surface. This was his domain.

By the following morning, Ken was regretting his petulance. He was cold and wet, he was frightened and he had absolutely no idea where he was (or where he was going). This was not progress; 24 hours previously he had been eating caramel popcorn[63] from a ceramic bowl on the sofa of a warm, dry house. He was acutely aware that his life was in something of a tailspin.

---

[63] This was a waste of good caramel; chickens can't taste sweet things. Caramel popcorn and feathers are **not** a good combination.

Ken was in a bush, shivering and thinking about food. His concussion was entirely gone and he was 95% chicken, but the humanity left in him knew how to be cute. When a mother with a pushchair strolled past, he hopped out and strolled along next to her. When she shouted "shoo", he turned his head to her and clucked. When she went a bit faster, so did he. When she stopped, so did he. When she asked him what he was doing[64], he clucked back at her as if in conversation. She gave Ken some of her croissant (jackpot) and when he hopped into the basket under the pushchair, she gave him a round of applause. If Ken had been blessed with the physical or mental capacity to bow, then he would have done so with gusto.

Back at home, Katharina made Ken feel at home by making him a nest in a laundry basket and installing him in a quiet corner of the utility room. The hum of the washing machine and the warm sun coming in through the window lulled him to sleep in a heartbeat and when he awoke, it was night again. It seemed sensible to investigate his surroundings and he systematically worked his way around every room of the house. There were a lot of rooms. The living room had a fluffy carpet that he wanted to roll around in, the kitchen was a sea of shiny (and slippery) marble that her could skate on and every other room was similarly exciting. Upstairs there were a multiplicity of rooms with closed doors and more bathrooms than Ken could count on the toes[65] of one foot. This was so much grander than that other house he had - by now - largely forgotten about. One of the doors

---

[64] She'd been on maternity leave for what felt like a lifetime. She had got so used to talking rubbish at her baby that she was prepared to coo at anyone or anything that replied. The chicken was the best company she was likely to have all day.

[65] They're probably called claws, rather than toes

was ajar and there were 'happy' noises coming from inside. Ken poked his innocent little chicken head through the door and saw Katharina dancing in bed. While Ken couldn't see the subject of her passions, he thought it looked fun.

It is probably not a surprise to you that an excited chicken is not a popular addition to any lovemaking session. In the throes of passion, Katharina's unsuspecting husband was caught off guard by an unsolicited peck to his pecker and his first response (after screaming like a stuck pig) was to grab Ken. He failed, and Ken tried to escape through a door that had closed behind him, leaving a handful of feathers and a trail of chicken-shit in his wake.

What followed was like a 1980s cartoon[66] where one animal chases another animal and unfeasible things happen to both of them. Ken's feet struggled to get any purchase on the laminate flooring so he found himself running on the spot quite a lot. Godfrey tripped over his own trousers on the floor. Ken did a commando slide under the bed and Godfrey ended up with a fresh handful of feathers. When Godfrey leapt over the bed (rugby style) to take Ken down, he did so with x-rated efficiency. If Ken had lived to describe the last thing he saw, nobody would have believed him. Just in case being flattened by the testicles of a stranger wasn't fatal enough, Godfrey threw Ken out of the open window, and that was that.

---

[66] Except one of the 'animals' was butt naked and sporting a raging erection…

Erica

It was loud, but Erica - being a chicken and a virtually embryonic one at that - had no real context of what 'loud' really meant. Or any other words, for that matter. She squeezed out of her oval casket and found herself pressing against something she would later find out was cardboard. She could see through a thin gap through to a room beyond. She knew this was a 'kitchen'[67] and the person she could see was cooking. As Erica watched in horror, she saw one of her siblings cracked open on the side of a glass bowl, then another and then another. As if this wasn't bad enough, the person then whisked them so thoroughly that it was impossible to differentiate one yolk from another.

Erica was too young (i.e. about 20 minutes old) to really understand what 'loss' was but she was afraid and sad and totally confused. In her emotional[68] state, she felt it was sensible to climb back under her shell and hide. Moments later, the box opened, and her closest neighbour was snatched away and turned to batter. Erica cowered under her egg-brella and prayed to the god of victoria sponges, hoping that no cake had more than 4 eggs in it.

She was in luck. Shortly after the massacre and some subsequent pouring, shaking and mixing, there was some clattering and then Erica felt movement. She saw light. She

---

[67] Remember - this is a totally ridiculous book about a sequence of chickens who are a tiny bit human. That's why she knew it was a kitchen. Get with the programme. Or program. I feel I should know which is which.

[68] Yes, chickens really do have emotions. In particular, they are capable of empathy. Who knew?

went towards the light[69]. She stopped moving, things went dark and suddenly she was chilly. No, not chilly... Actually cold. On reflection, 'cold' really wasn't a strong enough word; she was almost freezing. But not quite. She climbed out of her box onto a slidy surface. She slipped about a bit, walked into several things of different shapes and sizes, and smelled food. She ate some of the food she smelled, found something to wrap herself in[70], got as comfortable as she could and then waited.

Erica had no real concept of time, but it was nearly 24 hours later when Anton decided he needed a salad in his life. He opened his fridge and started choosing his salad ingredients. A handful of cherry tomatoes, half a cucumber, a red pepper and a very small lettuce. The ingredients were put on the kitchen worktop and one of the ingredients was cooled to the point where she was in a deep state of hyperthermia, wrapped in three increasing flaccid leaves. Anton cut the tomatoes in half, and the cucumber and pepper into batons. He laid them carefully onto his plate, whistling (badly) 'Je ne regrette rien'. He squirted some mayonnaise from a squeezy bottle and realised his life would not be complete without cheese. A small slice of brie and some Emmental appeared on his plate, arranged as though they were entering the 'cheese' category for London Fashion Week[71].

---

[69] No... not **that** light...

[70] Lettuce. Iceberg lettuce to be precise. She made an iceberg duvet. Oh, the irony...

[71] This is not a Thing. If it **were** a Thing, I would be much more inclined to partake in fashion, although my sandwiches would be the most fashionable thing I owned.

Erica was entirely unaware of the the whole cheese ensemble because she was a short waft away from a hyperthermic end. Luckily for her, Anton was so engaged in his dairy love affair that he forgot his lettuce and disappeared off to a quiet sofa to lust over his lunch. Also luckily for her, it was summer and really warm. The 'defrost' button had well and truly been pressed. In time, Erica regained consciousness and wriggled out of her lettuce blanket and into the shadow of an oversized pepper grinder. Her brain was still cold and slow and it took a while for her to get her bearings. She could hear sounds in another room and could see houseplants on a windowsill. There were an array of machines on the worktop and a shiny ceramic sink. This was a kitchen owned by a person who like to cook and who definitely knew how.

Anton returned to the kitchen and put his plate in the sink. He may as well not have bothered washing it because he had eaten every last morsel, but still he squirted, scrubbed and racked. In the process of washing up, he knocked a (very) sharp knife onto the floor. Erica couldn't really see what happened next but heard a

"MERDE!"

…followed by a lot of jumping about. The jumping about resulted in Anton succumbing to gravity and bouncing off his own marble floor. He stopped moving after that. Erica peeked out when she thought it was safe. There was blood on the floor, oozing consistently from the 6 inch blade that had gone through the front of his foot. Erica was strangely aware that this was both good and bad news; blood was never good news but bleeding feet were better than a bleeding head; it was all relative. Erica felt she ought to help but there's a limit to the medical capacity offered by a one day old chick. There was a pair of blue and red football socks hanging over the radiator, with 'LOSC' on them. Erica flapped down to the floor and hopped over to the radiator, leaving cartoon bloody footprints in a wobbly little line along the floor. She pulled the socks down and dragged them back to the motionless body on the floor. She wrapped the first sock tightly around the foot, and then tucked the toe end back into the top end to hold it in place. Then she did it again with the other sock. This simple action saved Anton's life; he would have undoubtedly bled to death in the six hours that he remained unconscious.

Satisfied that she had Done a Good Thing, Erica went off to investigate the rest of the house, underestimating both her energy levels and the sheer scale of the house, when exploring on one inch legs. She keeled over into a deep sleep about 4 metres away from Anton and woke up six hours later, a few minutes after he did.

He was a smart man and spotted the footprints despite his grogginess and pain. With his eyes, he followed them across the room to the fluffy yellow chick a few metres away and joined up all the metaphorical dots. He didn't understand (or believe) the story that this presented him with but the evidence was incontrovertible. He had been bandaged by a tiny chicken. It doesn't get weirder than that; was he high? Was he dead? At that moment the fluffball woke up, stared him dead in the eye, squeaked, and ran[72] away. Under normal circumstances he would have used his fabulously athletic body to gather Erica immediately, but the knife going through his foot turned out to be something of a

---

[72] No chicken ever really 'runs'. It's more like organised scrambling.

hindrance. He slipped a phone out of his back pocket, dialled 112 and waited.

"Ambulance…"

"…oui…"

"…maintenant…"

"…j'ai un couteau dans le pied…"

"…non, un couteau, pas Jacques Cousteau."

"…le pied…"

"…oui. Un couteau. Le pied. Un ambulance. Maintenant. Il y as beacoup de sang…"

"…trouver le bébé poulet."

"…poulet, oui."

"…jaune"[73]

…and then he passed out again. It was probably a conversation that would go down in paramedic history as the most ridiculous hoax call that wasn't a hoax call. Less than thirty minutes later, the designer front door was kindling and Anton was rushed into an ambulance amidst a breathy conversation:

"…c'est Anton!"

---

[73] Use Google Translate - I did. Other translation tools are available.

"Quel Anton??"

"Le footballeur"

"Mon dieu! Ne le laisse pas tomber!!"

Neenaw Neenaw Neenaw Neenaw Neenaw Neenaw Neenaw[74]

Erica finally felt like she was safe. She couldn't find a way out but she was slightly older and slightly bigger, so the stairs were achievable. She got up to the top, and made herself comfortable in the huge picture window on the landing so she could see anyone and anything that arrived at the house. After the sun had gone down and come back up again three times, she was hungry and really bored. Like, **really** bored. She branched out to one of the bedrooms, where she found - of all things - a knitting basket. She rolled several balls of wool out onto the floor and through some kind of ancient muscle memory did something with them that ended up looking loosely like a blanket. A very small blanket with lots of unintentional holes and a pattern that make normal human eyes bleed, but still a blanket. Erica dragged her handiwork back up onto the windowsill and made herself more comfortable. Less than an hour later, she was bored again. **Down**stairs is surely faster than **up**stairs, right? She stood at the top, leaned forward, then tucked herself into a little ball and bounced down every step until she landed at the bottom. She was wobbly for a while, but it had at least been a swift journey.

The next few days saw her learn several new skills that are largely not necessary in normal chicken life. Namely:

---

[74] If you can't work out what just happened, you shouldn't be allowed out unsupervised.

- Opening cupboards

- Turning on a tap[75]

- Pressing enough buttons on a remote control to make the TV work, but not enough to turn the volume down

- Opening a packet of crisps

- Operating a swing bin[76]

- Defrosting a freezer[77]

These things kept Erica fed and busy for exactly the length of time that it takes for a person to recover from a stab wound and severe concussion in a very expensive private hospital.

When Anton was discharged and chauffeur-driven back to his oversized house, the still-broken door was the smallest issue that he discovered. There was a hideous combination of blood, water, excrement and assorted foodstuffs covering a significant majority of the ground floor. This included both pure wool carpet and polished marble. His crutches did not cope well with the newly lubricated floor, so his progress was perilously slow. When he made his tearful journey upstairs and discovered wool, nests and more excrement in

---

[75] But not off. If she were more human she would have been interested to have discovered that the overflow outlet of a kitchen sink cannot keep up with the flow from a tap. In actuality, she just got really wet.

[76] This was accidental. She quickly learned that one could not roost on a swing bin.

[77] This was also accidental and added further moisture (and cost) to the catalogue of disasters that Anton was not yet privy to.

almost every room of his precious home, he descended into the depths of despair.

Let's be clear; Anton was fabulously wealthy by any scale you could possibly use. He had more money than any person could need and most people would baulk at his dismay following the wanton destruction of his home... but Anton wasn't 'that' kind of footballer. He had come from a dusty village in Cote D'Ivoire, had learned his trade in the absence of a school place, had seen two siblings die of malaria, and had been 'discovered' by pure fluke when he hit a ball squarely through the open rear windows of a Bentley parked by the roadside, on its way to a private villa by the sea. The passenger in the Bentley happened to be the manager of a football club and he knew talent when he saw it.

Anton had chosen to keep only 10% of his wages, from the moment he received them. He bought a four bedroom home with a lovely garden and upgraded it to a level of luxury he had never had the opportunity to even dream of before. By footballer standards, it was a modest home but by young chicken (and Anton) standards it was a palace. He had paid for a school and health centre to be built in his village, and had done everything he could to train all of its inhabitants in some way so that they could escape the poverty that fate had landed them in. He had upgraded homes, built toilets and laid water pipes. All of these things had been achieved quietly, for the good of the people and not for his own social media image. He was an actual hero.

Right now though, in this moment, surrounded by chicken shit and blood stains, he was at a historic low point in his life and not feeling like much of a hero. When Erica appeared in a doorway, he screamed at her in all of the languages he knew, none of which she understood. He threw stuff in her general direction, his athleticism overcome by emotion. She dodged them all, with uncharacteristically balletic skill. In his plunge to despair, he had knocked his crutch down the stairs, so he couldn't even hobble after her.

Seeing his predicament, Erica threw herself down the stairs and poked her head through the armhole of the crutch. With extraordinary effort and superhuman strength, she dragged the crutch up one step at a time until it was within reaching distance of the unhappy footballer. He took it and was then torn between beating her to death with it and hugging her. He did neither.

For several minutes, Erica did an uncomfortable little dance, where neither party quite knew what the protocol was. She didn't know what to say[78] and Anton was as high as a kite on a heady combination of painkillers combination and sleep deprivation. They avoided eye contact and wriggled about a bit until Anton broke the silence with an unexpectedly lengthy fart. Erica's feathers ruffled[79]. She turned and walked away into a bedroom with a suitably high perch that she felt safe on. Eventually, Anton wobbled through to her and babbled at her in French. Her French didn't stretch further than a recollection that 'Coq Au Vin' was bad news, so she cocked her head on one side in what she thought was an intelligent expression; Anton carried on talking.

---

[78] Partly because this was an awkward social situation that she just wasn't equipped for, but mainly because **she was a chicken**.

[79] This was involuntary; she wasn't being literally blown away by Anton's arse-song.

He was a busy soul, training a lot and doing a lot of Nice Things for the community that raised him. That meant that he had very few friends and nobody to snuggle up with at night; Erica was something to talk to, even if she didn't appear to understand a word he said.

A few days into the 'relationship', Anton was still babbling away, and in amongst what was like white noise to her, she heard something familiar…

"Blahblahblahblahblahblah un sandwich blahblahblahblahblahblah"… she looked up, and he noticed her interest.

"Tu veux un sandwich?" The upward inflexion at the end of his sentence told her that it was a question and she nodded.

He was excited; this was the first time he had seen any semblance of understanding in her behaviour and he leapt on it. For the next fifteen minutes, he held up a succession of potential sandwich ingredients, one at a time, announcing them in the kind of loud and deliberate way that one invariably speaks a foreign language to a native English speaker[80]. The human remnants of Erica's tiny brain began to recognise some of these things and as a result, her French vocabulary began to stretch:

'Du pain' - really squishy bread that you could go to sleep on.

---

[80] The implication always seems to be "You're too lazy or stupid to learn my language and I'm buggered if I'm learning yours, just because you think it's more important than mine… so I'm going to be loud and condescending instead. That'll teach you."

'Du fromage' - something that rich people refer to as 'cheese', which everyone else assumes is foot odour.

'Poulet' - **NOOOOOOOOOOOOOO!**

'Mayonnaise' - white goop that clogs your beak up

'Du beurre' - yellow goop that makes everything slippery

'Les Oignions' - Phoooweeeee. This will stay with you forever.

'Les saucisses' - yum but please cut it into smaller pieces...

'Moutard' - This held so much promise but... Ouch... Ouch... Ouch...

'Les oeufs' - wait... eggs are... you killed my family??

'Concombre' - Hmmmm. Kinda slimy but largely inoffensive. Winner.

'Les escargots?' - Now you're talking. This is like normal food but with added yum.

As the days went by, her vocabulary stretched beyond food and she began to find ways of responding; gesticulation[81], pointing at things around the house and animated responses to everything Anton said. She took small things to Anton as he convalesced in various parts of the house and he treated her to the things that she couldn't get to, which were mainly in the fridge. They were quite a team but Erica was aware that this wasn't really what Anton needed.

---

[81] Fairly limited without normal limbs and digits, but top marks for enthusiasm.

He needed human company and he needed people who didn't just see money when they looked at him. Erica decided to interfere through the medium of food...

Over the weeks that followed, she guided Anton - through his food delivery app - to order an astonishing variety of foods which catered for all tastes. She found that the more expensive ones were delivered by the people who made them rather than a delivery company, which seemed like an opportunity. One happy Thursday, the most beautiful lady Erica had ever seen arrived at the door with a beautiful Greek filo pastry dish, delicately shaped and perfectly cooked. Anton asked her lots of questions about it and she replied with increasing enthusiasm, although Erica didn't really understand what either of them were saying. They introduced themselves. She stayed for nearly ten minutes. As she turned to leave, Erica threw herself onto the ground with her feet in the air and squawked, and she came running back out of concern for the random chicken in the doorway. This prompted another conversation and they seemed to quite like each other. Erica miraculously recovered from her feigned collapse and the affair finished with ellipses rather than a full stop.

Two days later, she was back and she appeared to be called Thalia. She had bags full of shopping and was invited to the kitchen, where she and Anton spent hours discussing ingredients and marinades and cooking methods and seasoning until they had enough food for several football teams. They ate together and then sat in the living room and laughed together, but never got closer than a metre together; there was no suggestion of any kind of intimacy and Erica decided that this was unacceptable. She jumped up between them, took Anton's bright pink shirt and pulled him towards Thalia as hard as he could. They both found it hilarious and babbled away through their laughter but Erica clearly did not get the joke.

"Non, mon petit ami. Elle est une femme!" (cue more laughter)

These words were not in Erica's extremely limited vocabulary, but she was disappointed and very confused. Eventually, Thalia left, parting with a warm hug and a backward glance which Erica understood to be the start of something beautiful[82].

Every time Thalia came back, Erica's hopes were raised and dashed. She was not an expert in the intricacies of human romance, but she knew that she was looking at was **not** romance. They laughed a lot and talked a lot, which was essentially what Erica had been hoping for, but that was all.

One evening, Thalia bought a friend with her. He had beautiful hair and a huge smile, immediately fitting into their existing dynamic. When he sat next to Anton on the sofa, Erica felt that would get in the way of the Anton-Thalia thing, so she jumped onto his lap to squeeze out the biggest poo she could muster. He leapt up in horror and Anton shoed Erica away with one hand whilst ineffectually wiping with the other. This was not the outcome that Erica had hoped for. They went into Anton's room to find clean trousers and didn't come back for at least an hour. Erica assumed that they struggled to find a pair that fit properly, although she wasn't sure why Anton was wearing a different t-shirt when they re-emerged. Julian (the interloper) seemed to have

---

[82] Since you are more intelligent than an above-average chicken, you will have worked out that Erica was wrong.

entirely forgotten about his ordeal because he was grinning from ear to ear[83].

Julian kept coming back, and there seemed to be regular occasions where it was apparently necessary for one or other of them to 'get changed'. Then there was the kiss.

It was a passionate kiss, and not a lingering one.

It was accompanied by a close embrace and some stroking.

Erica was not familiar with the concept of LGBTQ+ relationships and her only other conclusion was that Julian must have been attacking Anton. This was compounded when they fell onto the sofa, tangled in a lustful moment that shut them out of reality for a while. There was thrusting and gyrating and all sorts of noises that Erica that didn't understand, but that she was sure were aggressive. At an opportune moment where there happened to be a gap between the two writhing bodies, she took a run-up and leapt between them with all claws out and beak down.

Erica's timing was not in her favour. She landed in Julian's groin at precisely the moment that Anton's sizeable pelvic region thundered down with all of its might.

The last thing that she saw was a the bulging zip on a very full pair of jeans, heading for her face. Julian required significant surgery for the intimate injuries that she inflicted in her dying moments, and Anton never ate chicken again.

---

[83] **Actually** grinning from ear to ear must surely mean a significant injury to the face

Nyle

There was rubbing. A lot of rubbing. Somewhere in the fluffy depths of his infant understanding, Nyle heard:

"Come on... come on buddy..."

Nyle **heard** the ellipsis, even though he didn't know any of the actual words. He opened his beady little eyes and his beaky little beak at the same time and coughed, or spluttered, or possibly even squeaked. The first thing he saw was a teardrop, hurtling towards his freshly opened eyes, a split second[84] before it smeared its salty torture into his brand new eyeball. You often hear that things were 'bad timing', but this literally couldn't have been worse[85]. Nyle lifted his hand to his face to wipe the tear away and became acutely aware that he had no hands on the ends of his arms[86], because yes, you've guessed it, he was a chicken.

Vigorous blinking got rid of the worst of his temporary blindness, and through fuzzy eyes he saw the concerned face of an adult, standing over him and - apparently - crying. The grin suggested these were tears of happiness, but Nyle wasn't immediately aware of what might have caused this happiness. The adult disappeared and came back dragging another adult, who wasn't crying. Together

---

[84] Not even a split second. A teardrop falls at around 10m/second, so it can only possibly have been about 0.15 of a second. Is there something smaller than a split second?

[85] Erica might have something to say about that.

[86] They are definitely legs and not arms, but this was a journey of understanding in which Nyle had not yet reached the destination.

they discussed Nyle in hushed tones[87] until one of them scooped him up and put him into a big metal bowl, covered in sawdust and with a light overhead. It was warm and cosy and there were lots of other small, fluffy, flappy entities waddling around nearby, bumping into each other frequently and generally looking like they were several hours into a rampant stag weekend. Nyle promptly fell over and went to sleep - it seemed the logical thing to do.

There was natural light filling the bowl when he woke up again, but the sides of the bowl were too high for him to see where the light was coming from. Some of his companions were also awake, so he struck up a conversation, which went something like this:

"Hey! Glad someone else is awake! Any idea where we go for breakfast around here?"

"Cheep"

"Well I should hope so - don't seem to have any pockets so not sure how I'm going to pay anyway! Reckon you could get mine?"

"Cheep"

"Alright - no need to be rude… What's your name anyway?"

"Cheep"

"Really? That's a weird name… What do your friends call you?"

---

[87] Why bother with the hushed tones? He was a chicken! You and I know that he was a sentient chicken but these anonymous adults didn't. That makes them just A Bit Weird.

"Cheep"

<Brief pause while Nyle's infant brain processed what he was hearing>

"...wait a minute. Is 'cheep' the only thing you can say?"

"Cheep"

Nyle ran[88] to the side of the bowl and looked at himself in its metal sides. He was disappointed to see that it was brushed aluminium and therefore as reflective as a black hole. Above him, the lamp hadn't yet sparked into action, and after a bit of wiggling, he got himself into a position where the angle meant he could see himself in the glass of the lamp.

"Arghghghghghghghghgh"[89]

This was the moment at which Nyle realised that he wasn't the man he thought he was, because men are rarely yellow and/or fluffy.

Nyle was inexplicably aware of psychology and the phrase 'fight or flight' sprung to mind. He felt immediately afraid and alarmed, as though he needed to be anywhere but where he was. He needed to get out of a metal bowl with 10cm sides when he had 2cm legs and entirely useless wings. He tried a running jump and achieved nothing more than a running thump. One of his co-prisoners was standing by the wall, and Nyle figured he could use him as a

---

[88] More of a waddle than a run but 'waddle' just doesn't portray the urgency with which he travelled.

[89] Again, this doesn't really do justice to the noise he made. It was the sound of a person screaming through the vocal chords of a chicken. I have literally no idea how you would spell that.

springboard, but only upgraded himself to a slightly higher running thump, with a longer attack from gravity afterwards. At that point it started raining concrete. It wasn't really concrete, but it was similarly hard and similarly painful on impact. Nyle ran to hide but there was literally nowhere to hide. As fast as it started, the attack stopped again. After a safety pause, Nyle went to investigate the 'rain' and it smelt good. So good.

Several 'raindrops' later, Nyle had eaten enough dried corn and went to sleep in a food-induced coma.

He woke up to a cacophony of squeaking, and a thin hand reached in and took one of the other chicks out of the bowl. A door closed, and that was that.

The cycle repeated several times: Eat - sleep - watch an abduction.

After the third chick disappeared (and none returned), Nyle's curiosity (combined with his intense desire to escape and general stupidity) made him spend the next few hours out in the middle of the bowl with his wings outstretched, making himself as visible and attractive as possible - acting on a wing and a prayer[90] - in the hope that next time it would be him who was lifted out of the bowl. Two days later, he was in luck, and it was him who was taken out on what he hoped would be a five star vacation somewhere in the Indian Ocean. He was very wrong.

---

[90] I did a funny!

The person who grabbed him studied his face, roughly pulled one of his wings out, and then threw[91] him into a bucket. In the bucket there was a writhing mass of other yellow fluffy things who all looked the same as him, but much more panicked. The more he looked, the more he saw, realising with horror that it was a really **big** bucket. He could hear voices beyond the bucket, but only just - there was a deafening machine-based noise going on in the background so he could only make out fractions of the conversation. There were two voices; one deep and one high pitched.

Deep: "Get... move... electric... money... NOW!"

High pitched (closer and slightly clearer): "But dad... cute... one... please?"

Deep: "Not... always...conversation... listen?"

High: "Promise... one... chores... pet?"

Deep (closer too): "One. And never again."

There was a squeal that signified either delight or the murder of a small beast. A little round face appeared at the top of the bucket and Nyle put on the best puppy dog face he could muster, which is difficult when you have none of the facial features of a dog. All of the fowl deities in the world were rooting for Nyle because the little round face was attached to a long, thin arm[92], which gently picked our

---

[91] Yes. Actually threw him. It wasn't a 'put' or 'drop' or a slightly clumsier 'plunk'. It wasn't even a nonchalant 'chuck'. It was a throw.

[92] Via a neck and shoulders

little hero up and popped him on a worktop. He turned to see the previous bucket upended into a very loud machine. Briefly, there was a tuneless orchestra of squeaking, some indescribable crunching, then a switch was pressed, and there was complete silence[93].

Nyle was no genius but he knew that his brothers would not be seeing another sunrise, and the man in him came gushing out in the form of imaginary tears[94]. He made a mournful noise which the little person next to him absolutely did not recognise as sad. She (or he - Nyle couldn't tell) picked him up by a wing and skipped out into the sunlight with his limp body flopping about by his/her side, like a spiky teddy bear that looks nothing like a bear.

After being spun around several times, dropped, thrown up in the air (and caught, thankfully) and kissed until he was beyond moist, Nyle was thrust into a miniature house in what he assumed was the child's bedroom. The child cackled for a few minutes, then skipped away again.

No chicken should understand the concept of surrealism, but clearly the human part of Nyle had a classical education and could appreciate the situation that he was in. He was a

---

[93] *Brief serious moment*. Male chickens aren't worth much because they can't lay eggs, so they are euthanised at 1 day old. Most institutions gas them, but some use a macerator, which is like an industrial blender. The chicks are thrown in alive and come out as a kind of paste. I don't really want to dwell on what happens to that paste, but I wouldn't like to speculate on where chicken nuggets **really** come from.

[94] Chickens have not magically formed tear ducts in the intervening chapters.

newborn chick, in a three bedroom mansion, with an ensuite bathroom and - he later discovered - a bidet[95].

All was quiet outside, so Nyle investigated his surroundings. Every room in the house seemed like it was designed to Nyle's exact proportions. He sat on each of the four chairs in the kitchen, one at a time. There was no particular reason; it just seemed like the right thing to do. He opened the 'oven' and there was a disappointing void inside. He would have tried the tap, but he had no hands. As he hopped out of the kitchen, he knocked a tiny mug off the table and onto the floor. It bounced, but never broke. Something to do with density, probably. In the living room there was a tiny sofa and two little cushions, all perfectly co-ordinated. Nyle sat on the sofa, then soon afterwards, he shat on the sofa[96]. He sproinged (and squelched) a bit, then tried to have a look up the chimney. There was nothing there and the fireplace didn't have a chimney, so he just hit his head. There was a carpet and exotic wallpaper. On the wall there was a tiny replica of the Mona Lisa. There was a tiny piano, but it didn't make any noise when Nyle pecked at it with his beak. There was even a conservatory, from which he could see out and into the bedroom in all directions. It was messy. Up the tiny staircase, he found three tiny bedrooms, each styled according to the scary doll that was resident.

The first bedroom was styled as a child's room. Specifically, it was the most stereotypically girly girl's bedroom in the history of bedrooms; there was so much pink that it made

---

[95] Let's just pause for a second. This is a child's doll's house. What designer in their right mind sits down at a drawing board to design a child's toy and thinks "Hmmm. What this child really needs is a scaled down arse-cleaning device. That'll make their childhood so very precious."

[96] Fowl have very little control over these things.

his eyes hurt. There was a tiny pink plastic desk with a tiny pink plastic chair. Sitting on the tiny pink plastic chair, upside down, was a tiny doll, dressed in pink. Nyle did not understand why the doll was upside down, but he was rapidly realising that there was a **lot** that he didn't understand. The pink bed was neatly made with a tiny pink duvet and a tiny pink pillow, but Nyle stopped paying attention after that because he frankly couldn't handle any more pink.

In the next bedroom, there was another horrendously stereotypical bedroom, but this time for a boy. Everything was - predictably - blue. This time the doll in the room was face down in bed, and blue; if it had been a real person, it would have suffocated. There was a tiny games console (not blue - shock!) and Nyle was disappointed to see that it was neither connected nor real. There were some tiny blue clothes on the floor and a tiny blue rug, shaped like a shark. The third bedroom was apparently the 'master suite', with a full set of bedroom furniture and an ensuite shower room. There was a naked doll in the shower, and Nyle felt he should look away, although it was a child-friendly doll with no discernible genitals of any kind. Its arms were up in the air as though it was being held at gunpoint and it had a dead stare on its face. The final room was the family bathroom, complete with bath, shower, toilet and bidet. Nyle didn't know what a bidet was, but it was a more comfortable perch than the toilet.

By this point, Nyle had done a lot of hopping, and it's exhausting being a one day old chick. He made his way back into the master bedroom and tucked himself under the duvet to sleep. Anyone looking in would have undoubtedly said "Awwwwww" if they saw him, with nothing but his little beak poking out of the top as he slept soundly, dreaming of corn and porcelain.

When he woke up, invigorated, it was a new day. Downstairs, he found water in the little cup (which had been replaced on the table) and a few pieces of corn on a plate on the table. A tiny vase of plastic flowers had been put on the table and he felt like a king. He did all of the things that he'd done the previous day, going from room to room and testing the furniture, but most of it was only for show so he very quickly got bored.

Plan number 1 was to climb out of the window, but the window was made of glass, which came as a (painful) surprise.

Plan number 2 was to climb up the chimney, but of course the chimney wasn't really a chimney.

Plan number 3 was to try all of the other windows, stupidly assuming that they would be any different to the first.

Plan number 4 did not exist.

Nyle planted himself on the bottom step and contemplated his own misery. For some time, he stared down the hall into the nothingness of his existence and - after more time than he would have cared to admit - he realised he was actually looking at the front door. The door. Why wasn't this plan number 1?[97] An actual door?

One little chicken foot opened the tiny door, and out he fell into the outside world. He would like to have **stepped** out

---

[97] This is a rhetorical question; he was, let's not forget, a chicken, after all.

into the outside world, but the dolls house was on the edge of a table, so he stepped out into nothing and once again succumbed to gravity. There was so much to explore in this new world - dirty clothes to sniff (error), toys to climb around in and balls to balance on (and fall off). He cavorted for a while, but was ripped from his nirvana by voices downstairs. His urge for self preservation told him to flee back to his little house, and after some laundry mountaineering he made it back and was able to install himself at the table expectantly just in time for his next meal. More corn. Yay.

For the next 4 weeks (give or take), this was the pattern of his life. Every inch of the bedroom had been explored and every inch of the doll's house had been shat on. His 'owner' didn't seem to have much regard for hygiene, given the state of the laundry and the apparent inability to pursue a basic dolls house cleaning regime. It was a well appointed dolls house but it was bereft of cleaning products and there was certainly no steam cleaner for miniature carpets.

At the end of week 4, Nyle woke up and realised his feet were sticking out of the bottom of the duvet. When he walked through the doorways of the house, he had to stoop. When he escaped through the front door, he had to breathe in. When he tried to balance on the tiny kitchen chairs, he invariable fell off, as a result of his sizeable arse. He had become a man[98]; it was time to leave home. It was also time to have something other than corn for dinner.

The main bedroom door was always closed, so he had to find somewhere near the door to hide, hoping to escape at the first opportunity. His chosen den was an overturned

---

[98] Well not a man exactly, just not a chick anymore, but a chicken who felt like an adult man.

welly[99], which looked out at the door. After a short weight[100], his captor burst through the door with the jubilance of excitable youth. Some corn was carefully placed on the tiny table, a nose was wrinkled at the smell in the house, and that was his chance. He scuttled out through the open door and began his journey down the stairs as fast as his legs would throw him.

Unfortunately for Nyle, that wasn't very fast.

"Come to Mari…"

Was it a threat or a statement of fact? Nyle wasn't sure but he was only on the second step so it was hardly a surprise that he'd been caught. Mari took him back into the bedroom and tried to return him to the dolls house, but he took the initiative to make himself as big and floofy as possible, so that it was clear he wouldn't fit through the door. Mari decided that every house needed a rooster on the roof, and obediently perched Nyle on top of the house. It was an improvement on being stuck inside the house, but only just. Mari babbled away at him for a while. There was every possibility that Nyle understood every word, but he didn't care enough to pay attention. For all he knew, Mari could have told him how to escape, or whispered the answer to everything in his little ear. All Nyle heard was:

"Blahblahblahblahblahblah. Blah? Blahblahblah!"

Then she left.

---

[99] Who keeps wellies in their bedroom? Unruly farm children with no concept of personal hygiene. That's who.

[100] Yes, I know this should be 'wait' and not 'weight' - I just wanted to know if you were paying attention. Well done if you were.

Now he was a bit bigger, Nyle's wings had become very slightly bigger and very slightly less useless. He was still a long way away from anything that you might describe as 'flying' but at least he could put up a brave fight against the forces dragging him down, and land slightly more gracefully[101].

There was a window. The window was closed. There was a door, which was also closed. As he slouched around the room looking exactly like whatever a teenage chicken looks like, his literary juices were stirred by the books strewn liberally around the floor. He chose one, lay on the floor and kicked it open with his feet, and sat down to read.

He was a little surprised to discover that 'reading' was in his skillset[102].

"Dicky was a ducky, swimming in a pool.
He wanted to go walking, but felt like such a fool!
Dicky saw a doggy, dwindling by a bog,
And ran out to the doggy, who was chatting to a frog.
They all went for a wander, to see what they could see,
A fishy and a butterfly, a small mouse and a bee.
The bee went buzzy buzzy, the mouse wrinkled its nose,
Froggy had a camera, and Dicky struck a pose.
They all walked off together, and climbed into a truck..."

Nyle didn't turn the next page, because he didn't give a f...

---

[101] I use the word 'gracefully' with a significant chunk of artistic license here.

[102] In case you've forgotten, the faint premise of this ridiculous story is that this a chicken who is part person. Remember? It is therefore entirely logical that this chicken can read. Duh.

What was this drivel that children were filling their heads with? Since when did a duck on a road trip count as literature? It was at this point that Nyle decided he would make it his life's work to write a book to rival 'Dicky the ducky'. There were some coloured pencils on the floor and some drawing paper; what better time than now?

Nyle tried to pick up a pencil with his hands, but his hands were still wings and they barely even met each other. He picked the pencil up with his beak, and tried to write, but wasn't flexible enough to bend his neck to 90° so that he could stand and write at the same time. He tried to lie on his side and write by scrambling around with his feet to move himself around on the paper. This is what he wrote:

Caption

This was not exactly Moby Dick.

He tried holding the pencil in his feet, with a tiny bit more success; with much huffing and puffing and intense concentration, he managed to write

BORED

This was as much as he had the energy to write. It was a start, but a bit of mental maths flagged up that his life's work would take him several lifetimes to write[103]. There had to be another way... Which landed in his lap in no time; by chance, Mari was gifted a laptop for her birthday that very week. Once she set it up in her room, Nyle was able to watch her log in and learn her password. She had clearly been absent for her token 'online safety' lesson, because her password was 'password'.

Nyle was free to log in and reap havoc, subject to internet filters and beak tiredness. He was just about big enough to stand just below the space bar and reach all of the keys with his beak, jumping on the space bar when necessary. He briefly experimented with foot and wing typing but it was a disaster. Whilst using his face gave him the typing score of an elderly gentleman painstakingly writing their memoirs with glaucoma and only one (arthritic) finger, was not accurate and much less tiring than leaping from key to key. He had limited time while Mari was out of the room, but he got faster as time went on, and advanced from one paragraph per day to one page per day after a week of practice. He saved his file under the incognito filename 'Fowl homework' in a folder somewhere subtle[104], and after a few weeks he'd amassed 15,000 words. He Googled a literary agent, set up an email account and sent them an email offering them a sample of his work. He sent it. They

---

[103] It would take him 764 days of solid writing, at a rate of 20 minutes per word. With this kind of exertion, he'd be dead by the end of the first paragraph.

[104] Yes - there is a definite continuity issue here. When and where did Kyle learn about appropriate file storage and folder organisation? We'll just put it down to 'it was the but of human in him' as that covers a multitude of sins.

were impressed. Several months[105] later, his work was complete and he sent the finished article to his agent.

What came next took the world by storm. Nyle gave himself a pen name of 'Chiquita Cockton', set up a bank account[106], and watched his royalties come rolling in. His first book was about a child who made a daring escape from prison, and it shot straight to the top of the bestseller list. His agent emailed him some of the reviews:

"Such a fresh new perspective on life"

"Empathy on a whole new scale!"

"Almost feels like a farm animal talking about being trapped. Inspiring."

By this stage, Nyle had graduated from the roof of the dolls house because he was too big; he perched on the windowsill instead and had lost all interest in escaping, given his successful new career. His second book was also a runaway success, and his bank balance was bursting at the seams. Whilst writing a book generally isn't all that lucrative, his outgoings were non-existent; partly because he had no way of spending it and partly because realistically there was nothing that he needed to buy. He was almost fully grown and could type remarkably fast but his limited

---

[105] This was all he had going on in his life. It's amazing what you can achieve when all you have in your life is a laptop and a dirty welly.

[106] Please suspend your disbelief at this point. I know he couldn't possibly have done this, because you need ID documents and an address etc to set up a bank account, and no chicken has a passport and 5 years of address history to fall back on. Cut me some slack here - it's only a bloody story.

life experience meant that he was running out of material for his third book, in what his agent had decided should be a trilogy. Like Banksy, he'd managed to keep his identity secret and avoid all meetings, interviews and articles. He'd claimed to have a phobia of phones and people and this had become part of his charm.

By the time he started book number 3, Nyle's creative juices had run dry. His story had seen the boy escape from his first prison, only to get trapped in another. The second book saw him out in the real world, but in hiding. What could happen to him next? What might make a good storyline? Nyle stood at the window and watched the farmyard below for hours and hours, searching for inspiration. It came in the form of a Lamborghini which gingerly[107] pulled up one Saturday afternoon. His escapee could become a racing driver and win lots of races! He wrote his third book, submitted it, and then sat back to watch the money roll in. The editing process seemed longer than it had with the other two, and there was a degree of reluctance to publish… but who can argue with such a successful author?

The agent should have trusted his gut. The storyline was absolute bollocks which made no sense. Chiquita Cockton's loyal readership dropped him like a pair of pants in a dysentery outbreak and his bank balance stayed stubbornly stable. His career was over as fast as it had begun, and Nyle was once again bored out of his beak. It was time to fledge and fly the coop[108].

---

[107] A Lamborghini has about 8cm of ground clearance, and farmyards have potholes. Enough said.

[108] Again - this is figurative. He couldn't fly and he wasn't in a coop.

The door was too obvious an escape route and had failed him before. He found the heaviest thing he could (an encyclopaedia) and hurled it at the window, relieved to see that the window was not double glazed, and surprised by his unexpected understanding of the physical properties of a double glazed window. The encyclopaedia-sized[109] hole in the window was conveniently small-chicken-sized too, and out he popped. From the windowsill, he could see the ground, and it was a long way away. It would have been a long way away to a person, but to a chicken it was even further. He looked. He contemplated. He wussed out and stepped back inside. He ruminated on his options and looked around him at what his life had become - the festering laundry, then increasingly crusty dolls' house and the tatters of his fledgling career, then took a running jump at the window without a backward glance. He was - briefly - flying. It was the most perfect moment, which really did happen in slow motion. What was probably less than ten seconds took up about ten minutes in his head as he basked in the ruffling of his feathers, the sun on his face, the farmyard below... he felt free. Sadly, it was the briefest sensation of bliss that he would ever feel, broken up in an instant by the immediacy with which he was heading for the ground.

Before he really had the time to think about the best place to land or how to roll like a ninja, he hit the ground. There was no fortuitous puddle or haystack like there is in the movies, just a lawn. A lawn after a heatwave; a very hard lawn. Scientific research shows that cats are evolved to spin in the air, so that - as long as they're falling far enough - they always land on their feet. In 1894, Etienne-Jules Marey

---

[109] Like diarrhoea and haemorrhage, encyclopaedia is a stupid word,

used slow motion photography to examine what a cat does when it rights itself; they have excellent balance and 30 vertebrae which enable them to turn their feet downwards when they fall from a height up to 60m. Even from this height, cats can survive without serious injury.

All of this is fascinating, but for Nyle there were two major issues:

1. He didn't know any of it.

2. He wasn't a cat.

With a measly 15 non-flexible vertebrae and really shitty balance, Nyle hit the ground arse first and bounced very slightly. His tail was unmistakably broken and the subsequent bounce gave him an origami wing. It hurt. Miraculously, his feet were intact and he was able to amble away into a bush to contemplate his next move and lick the wounds he didn't have with the tongue that didn't exist, poking out of a mouth that couldn't reach anyway.

What was his next move? He was loose in a world that he only knew through a non-proprietary search engine that nobody has ever heard of. As most internet warriors are, he was misguided to an incredible degree and knew a negligible amount about a huge number of things. He knew enough about the world to make himself sound clever in a short conversation but moronic if it turned into anything more than idle chit-chat[110]. He looked at the lawn in front of him and a multitude of ill-considered hazards fled across his mind:

---

[110] Since he was a chicken and incapable of human speech, these scenarios were unlikely to ever become an issue.

- What if the wolves could smell him?
- Were there sharks in the pond?
- Would MS-13 be waiting for him?
- Would he be able to speak Esperanto when it came to it?
- Would he be able to breathe the air for long enough?
- Would he escape the paparazzi when he got into the big city?
- Would he be able to handle the advances of the screaming women who would hurl themselves at him?
- Would the Lizard People be ready to pounce?
- Would he suffer third degree burns from a coffee purchased at a well-known food retailer, and spend several months in complex litigation hearings?
- What if his Pisces was rising in Aries?
- Would he get fat and never work again following his miraculous pregnancy?

These are the paranoid concerns of an entity that gained the majority of its world view from reading tabloid newspapers online. All of these things filled him with dread and he could barely set one foot in front of the other, so he retreated further into a bush and did was he was 'reliably' informed was called building a lair[111], then went to sleep. He woke up in the dark, which totally screwed up his concept of time and his ability to see. With renewed bravery, he stepped out into the perilous world before him, puffed out his chest, stood up to his full 21cm[112] height and marched off into the wilderness. His proud march took him about 400m to the end of the garden, where he was foiled by a fence. He built a new 'lair' under a new bush, and waited for the sun to come up again.

---

[111] He wasn't. He was roosting. Not even nesting.

[112] If you're over 50, that's about 8 inches.

Some time around 8.45[113], a van pulled up at the front of the house. A man in a hat with a resting bitch face[114] and an ill-fitting hoodie stepped out, with a package in one hand. He went to the door, pressed the bell, waited for a millisecond, then stepped to the side and hurled his package down the garden 'for safety'. It landed behind a bucket, where nobody was likely to see it, and he sauntered back to his van, whistling tunelessly. When the coast was clear, Nyle crept over to the bucket to investigate the delivery. Our plucky little hero dragged the small parcel to the front door with his broken wing flapping loosely behind him, and casually had the Eureka moment that he needed. In order for his new plan to succeed he would need to get back into the house.

Mari arrived home from school the next day and threw the front door open with reckless abandon. Nyle hopped in behind her and his next adventure began. He followed her up the stairs; in his head he was like 007 but in reality it was much less exhilarating than that and he was lucky that she didn't hear his indelicate thudding on the stairs[115]. Mari was apparently not that bothered that her pet chicken had disappeared into thin air and her mourning didn't stretch beyond a shrug. Nyle was able to hide in her bedroom until she was gone again, so that he had free rein to use the laptop. He logged into his online banking account and was pleased to see that it had swelled to a whopping

---

[113] This was a complete guess. Where would a chicken put a watch??

[114] This is a phrase generally applied to women; there is no male equivalent. Resting git face? Resting miserable bastard face? Resting twat face? The possibilities are endless but for the sake of the already bulging Oxford English Dictionary, let's just make 'bitch' a male/female hybrid term.

[115] Fortunately, Mari was both heavier and less graceful than Nyle.

£49,012.26. As he watched, his page refreshed and went up to $49,013.76. His next action was the stroke of genius...

The package in the garden had reminded Nyle that he had a source of income, a delivery driver who was truly awful and an address; the perfect storm for an incognito online shopping spree. For safety, he used Mari's name on the account, so that it was believable, and logged went straight to www.borneo.co.uk[116].

And so began a £3,326 spree of buying (mostly) absolute shite.

- A dog's suit and tie, which he hoped would also fit a chicken.
- A phone and a solar phone charger
- A rubber chicken, so he didn't feel alone
- A large remote-controlled car
- Caramel coated popcorn
- A half bottle of champagne, which he then had to cancel as he had no proof of ID
- A hand/beak held computer game thingy
- A small kennel
- A very small blanket
- A torch[117]
- An electric blanket

---

[116] If you know anything about geography, you will understand what this is a reference to. If you know anything about the law, you will understand why I have used an imaginary online shop.

[117] Nyle had a partially human brain, but he wasn't the sharpest knife on the rack. Everyone needs a torch - that's common knowledge. It's also fairly common knowledge that limbs are significant in holding onto the torch and therefore using it.

- A 42" TV[118]
- A small laptop and portable wifi gadget
- A small bag of corn
- A 65 piece cutlery set
- Dog shoes[119]

After he hit 'pay now', Nyle could almost see his sparkling future mapped out in front of him. He lay back on the chair (briefly, before remembering he had a broken tail) and dreamed of driving around in a suit, eating popcorn and listening to his favourite tunes on the phone by his side, sad that there was no such thing as sunglasses for chickens. His happy dream was interrupted by an unfamiliar noise downstairs.

Woofwoofwoofwoof. Arooooooooorgh.

Nyle thought quickly; he had no idea what flavour of dog it was and how much of a threat it posed to him, but in his head all dogs were slavering wolves who would rip his throat out in the blink of an eye. Mari's parents' repair of the smashed window showed as much concern for DIY as they had for climate change, and Nyle was able to rip off the corrugated cardboard and brown tape with very limited effort. Like any sentient chicken (!), he had learned from his

---

[118] Another stroke of not-so-genius. In his excitement, he hadn't planned for how he would move the TV, where he would plug it in, or how it would fit in the kennel that he also had nowhere to put. 48 hours later, Mari was overwhelmed by the anonymous gifts that were delivered to her.

[119] It's a sad indictment of the world in which we live, that dog shoes are A Thing. I'm sure some dog owners out there will be incandescent with rage, with a billion reasons why their precious pooch needs shoes. My transient knowledge of dog anatomy suggests that Dogs Don't Need Shoes. Or boots, or sandals or any kind of footwear at all, **BECAUSE THEY'RE DOGS.**

mistakes and was not prepared to break another wing. He gathered the corners of a pillowcase together as a makeshift parachute, held them together in his beak, and then took his chances with gravity once again.

Anybody with a cursory understanding of aerodynamics, parachuting or pillowcases, will know that this strategy was doomed to fail. He let go of one corner, for a start, and the remaining material was more of a sail than a parachute, which was his one success and his first stroke of luck for a while. He was propelled far enough outwards that his resting place was a trampoline, which he hit face first (piercing it and destroying Mari's future trampolining career) then bounced off into a bush. If he had been in a cartoon, it would have been hilarious and would invariably become a GIF for all eternity.

But he was safe, with no further injuries and a renewed respect for gymnastics. He retreated to his corner and absentmindedly looked for worms.

The next day, the first consignment of Nyle's order was delivered with the expected level of care. Anything which was lobbable was lobbed. Everything else was left in a heap. It was up to Nyle to try and move it all before anyone came home and destroyed his dream.

One package at a time, he dragged his booty to the end of the garden. Not everything had been available on 'next day delivery', which was a blessing in disguise; there was no way he could have moved it all. As he surveyed his new life, wrapped in cardboard and glistening brown tape, he began to consider the merits of thinking things through before acting on a whim. On further reflection, he reconsidered his purchases:

- A dog's suit and tie, which he hoped would also fit a chicken.
  - *It didn't. He didn't have enough limbs or a neck that filled the neck hole. Nor did he have the thumbs required to deal with buttons.*
- A phone and solar charger
  - *Touchscreen phones require fingers, which are in short supply on chickens. Capacative touchscreens require skin to touch them, so he couldn't use it for anything. Modern phones have zero buttons.*
- A rubber chicken, so he didn't feel alone
  - *It was modelled on a dead chicken, thoroughly plucked. It made Nyle very uncomfortable.*
- Caramel coated popcorn
  - *This was incredible. A small success in a sea of failure, although when it stuck to his feathers it **really** stuck to his feather.*
- A small kennel
  - *Great in principle, but flat-packed. With no hands to hold the pieces and no screwdriver to put the pieces together with, it was absolutely no use at all. He hoped that he might find a way to build it, but on face value it was another expensive disaster.*
- A very small blanket
  - *Another small win, until it was rained on and became so wet and heavy that it was no use to man nor chicken.*
- A torch[120]
  - *No further detail required.*

---

[120] Nyle had a partially human brain, but he wasn't the sharpest knife on the rack. Everyone needs a torch - that's common knowledge. It's also fairly common knowledge that limbs are significant in holding onto the torch and therefore using it.

Nyle felt that his next foray into the world of internet shopping would be more fruitful but for now all he had was some very nice popcorn.

One more full rotation of the Earth passed, and the worlds' worst delivery driver once again dropped his load somewhere near the front door. He couldn't even be bothered to throw anything this time and was clearly in a hurry to ruin someone else's day, which was good news for Nyle.

A rundown of his second delivery:

✦ An electric blanket
  ✦ *Fairly useless without a power supply, but dry at least.*
✦ A 42" TV
  ✦ *Too big, too heavy and too electric. Happy Thursday, Mari.*
✦ A small laptop and portable wifi gadget
  ✦ *Useful for as long as the precharged battery lasted, which was 26 minutes. Long enough to discover that the solar charger bought for the phone was only powerful enough for a very slow trickle-charge, which would take days to charge it to full use... but it was better than nothing.*
✦ A small bag of corn
  ✦ *Better than worms, not as good as caramel popcorn.*
✦ A 65 piece cutlery set
  ✦ *Even Nyle was baffled by this. He wasn't a magpie, attracted to shiny things[121]. He had no hands with which to hold cutlery, nor plates to put food on. There*

---

[121] This is a myth, anyway; magpies couldn't give two shits about shiny things. They steal stuff sometimes and are generally pretty clever, but shininess is not a quality they value.

wasn't even any comedy value in a well made Sheffield spoon.
- Dog shoes
  - *Nyle was acutely aware that he was not a dog. On inspection, he discovered, to his dismay, that he did not have dog's feet, nor did he have opposable thumbs with which to tie the ridiculous shoe laces on his ridiculous shoes.*
- A large remote-controlled car
  - *Great in theory, requiring a 240v plug in practice.*
- A hand/beak held computer game thingy
  - *Designed for people with hands; the clue's in the name. He could just about hold it with his feet, but when he hit the buttons with his beak, he couldn't see the screen at the same time. As a result, he died in every game he played.*

So. There was a small amount of progress. The laptop had enough charge for another order that very evening, and he made much more sensible decisions this time around. He ordered a small set of tools, some batteries and an extension lead, and waited.

Fast forward to the same time the following day, and Nyle was (very slowly) building a small wooden kennel behind a bush at the end of the garden, with very little skill. He had to lean all of the pieces up next to each other and then screw them together with his feet, which meant that he couldn't hold them together at the same time. None of the screws were in properly, nothing was straight and the end product did not sit flat on the floor. Despite all of that, the roofing felt that came with it made it watertight, and it was a lot warmer and drier than being outside. He put the electric blanket inside, ran an extension cable into the garage through a cat flap, and snuggled into a warm night's sleep after an exhausting day.

Nyle dreamed of being massaged under the sunshine of a Caribbean island. He was strangely moist but so calm and happy that it almost seemed real. When the tongue of a dachshund licked his eyeball, he discovered the true horror of his situation. The giant wolf he had heard downstairs was in fact the monster before him. Teeth[122] glinted in the morning sun. A tail like a cosh whipped backwards and forwards, inflicting untold damage on Nyle's battered body. Giant eyes stared into his very soul and he feared for his life. The wolf[123] covered the only exit from his home, and Nyle lay frozen in fright, unsure what his next move could possibly be. He was sniffed. There was a peculiar noise:

"Rrrroooff?"

It wasn't a bark and it wasn't a howl, but it wasn't exactly menacing. The little head was cocked slightly to one side, in a way that said 'I want to be your friend and I don't know how'. Kyle jumped to his feet and the wolf ran away, clearly far more scared than he was. So scared, in fact, that he left a little pellet of his own fear on the floor in the doorway. Kyle poked his head out and saw the dog cowering on the other side of the garden - visibly shaking. This was a rare streak of good news and Nyle felt he could have an ally in this ridiculous creature. He offered the dog - now named Wolfy - some of the remaining popcorn and Wolfy became his best friend before the popcorn was even on the floor.

---

[122] It was a puppy. They weren't even very big teeth.

[123] There is no reality in which a sausage dog puppy is anything like a wolf, but Nyle was't very clever.

Together, they sat and contemplated the world. Every time Nyle moved, Wolfy leapt to his feet expectantly, with his unfeasibly long tongue lolling to one side and his little eyes full of love and excitement. At no point did he realise that Nyle was unable to throw a ball, nor did he have any real food. Wolfy was really dumb, but very cute, and very attentive to Nyle. His allegiance flipped the second a human came home; Wolfy sprinted[124] back to the people with toys, food and a sofa.

Nyle used a tiny screwdriver to painstakingly remove the back cover on the remote control of his car; chickens are not designed for holding screwdrivers, so it took a while. He then plugged the car into the extension cable running into the garage, and charged it up. It wasn't a car designed for passengers, but Nyle was only small, and could just about squeeze inside. He had paid extra for a car that was an accurate model, which meant there was a back seat which he could load up with food, a blanket, and his functional electronics. Nyle's escape plan was almost ready to spring into action - he just needed to say goodbye to Woolfy.

This was a fairly pointless endeavour; neither Woolfy nor Nyle could speak or understand words, and Woolfy didn't really care who he was with, as long as they had food. He would not miss Nyle at all, and Nyle knew it - especially once he saw the bottom of the popcorn packet. The next day, he gave Woolfy the pointless dog shoes[125], scrambled

---

[124] I use the term loosely. Dachshunds have incredibly short legs and therefore make very little progress even when their legs are working flat out. It's probably cruel to laugh at them, but it's hard not to.

[125] Woolfy, who had not gained any notable grey matter in the intervening hours, ate them.

into his car, and remote-controlled himself off down the road.

A few cars beeped at him.

A small child squealed as he pootled by.

Nyle was on an adventure and nothing was going to stop him. Nothing, that is, apart from the battery life of his car. After less than half a mile, there was no juice left in the tank and Nyle was overjoyed to be at the top of a long hill which might buy him some more distance. It was a straight road, which was handy because he hadn't factored in the need for the car to have batteries, in order to change direction with the remote control. He also hadn't factored in a lack of brakes, or the dual carriageway at the bottom of the hill. Nyle met his maker courtesy of a tourbus carrying a lesser-known rock band on the final leg of their European tour.

All that was left to mark Nyle's short existence was a canteen full of cutlery in a badly built kennel. Ironically, his book sales went through the roof once he disappeared.

Brian[126] and Betty

"Ow"

"Ooof"

"Eeee"

"Mfff"

These were all noises that Brian and Betty would have made if they had vocal chords, and had been born. Trapped inside one shell, there was no room to move and it was unpleasant and uncomfortable, but fortunately for them they would never have any memory of any of it. Tragically, they were also facing each other, so when they had the natural urge to peck their way out of their shell, all that actually happened was a mutual blinding in one eye as they mauled each other in an accidental attack. As is the case with most twin chickens borne of a double yolk, Brian and Betty were destined to die. Had they been head to toe, or facing outwards, they would have had a chance but they weren't.

---

[126] It is worth noting that, had Brian been a person, over half of the people in his life would have regularly written his name as 'Brain'. Most would have been accidental, some ignorant and some undoubtedly thought they were being hilarious. Every Brian in the world knows that they would be sadly mistaken.

Fortunately for these two beauties, Alectryon[127] was looking down on them with a smile, and they burst out of their shell with far more energy than is usual, mainly because their survival was the result of having been born on a shelf, and rolling off that shelf as a result of in-ovo bickering that made the egg wibble off the edge and fall far enough to crack.

Brian and Betty lay in the straw and stared at each other with a strange hybrid of love and hate, reserved only for siblings. It's the same emotion that means you can fight each other to the death, but would also defend each other to the death if someone else tried to get in on the action. Nobody is allowed to beat the crap out of your siblings, except you; it's a universal fact that crosses the cultural divide and is a feature of every society on earth[128]. They were both blind in one eye, having fought even before they were born, but fortunately it wasn't the same eye. If they stood side by side, they would be able to see in both directions if they worked as a team.

They stood up. The looked around the new world that they had been born into. It was a shed, and there was only one other bird around, which a process of elimination suggested was their mother. She jumped majestically[129] from her perch to rescue them, and snuggled up with them; there were no other noises from the shelf so it seemed they were her only

---

[127] Alectryon is genuinely the Greek god of chickens. There are a lot of religions out there, so there's a god for almost everything - you just have to do a lot of research before you do any praying and frankly that's just too much effort for something that's almost certainly made up anyway. Sorry, Alectryon - please don't send a giant rooster to smite me.

[128] This may be complete bollocks, but it's true of most of the siblings I know so I'm going to call it Science.

[129] No she didn't. Nothing that a chicken does is majestic.

offspring. What Brian and Betty didn't know was that she'd laid them on a shelf so that they didn't get stolen away like all of her other eggs; it was paramount that the humans didn't see them and flush them down the toilet or feed them to the dog. She used her feet to fashion a crater in the straw and gently poked them until they were hidden in it, then she sat on them. They were warm, and then they were asleep.

The kerfuffle of feeding time woke them up and they had their first meal. It was like the rest of their meals were likely to be for whatever remained of their lives; a compressed mass of mushed up grains. Probably better in flavour and/or nutritional value than corn but no more exciting. They were still very small, and could stay hidden under the straw, which - unbeknownst to them - was a blessing.

As time went on and they grew, their capacity to hide began to diminish. A heap of straw was piled on top of them but it was starting to look distinctly like a nest, so it was time to change the plan. Their mum was 100% chicken and therefore had a brain the size of a marble, but they - through whatever tenuous thread is holding this storyline together - had a degree of human thought. They knew they were in trouble.

There is a huge amount of anecdotal evidence that twins have a connection beyond that of other siblings. They make the same choices when apart, sometimes feel each others' emotional or physical pain, and seem to have a deeper perception of each others' thought processes than other siblings or friends. There's not enough research to explain or even confirm this, but it's what most twins say, so there's probably a degree of truth in it. For Betty and Brian, it would be the myth which proved to be factual enough to save their lives on an almost daily basis.

Let's recap. Chickens can't talk, but part-human chickens[130] think in words that they simply don't have the biological capacity to share with the world. Some form of ESP, therefore, is immensely helpful. Brian and Betty **knew** what was going on in each others' heads, without making so much as a 'peep'[131]. It meant that they made quite a team, and could perform extraordinary feats that most chickens weren't even capable of considering.

In this instance, it meant they were able to use each other to get up to one of the rafters of the shed that they were in. As we have established on several occasions, chickens do not fly; they simply fall slightly slower than a brick and with a lot more noise. Betty and Brian experimented with throwing themselves towards the rafters with various combinations of flapping and scrabbling, but - contrary to the 1980s number one hit[132] - the only way was down. The shed, however, was made of slatted wood, and the lower edges of the slats were enough for a chicken to briefly hold on to.

If Brian could get a grip on a slat, turn backwards and grab his sister with his beak and hurl her upwards, she could then return the 'favour' and they could work their way up the wall as if they were climbing a ladder. The whole process had to be performed quickly though because it was impossible to hold on for more than a second or two, which meant a lot of failed attempts before they made it to the top.

---

[130] That's still not a Thing. You and I both know that, but it's what this story is about, so deal with it.

[131] Farmers often call tiny chicks 'peeps' because that's the noise they make. Cute.

[132] For anyone born after 1980, this is a reference to 'Yazz and the Plastic Population' performing 'The Only Way is Up'. You should look it up; you'll be humming it for days and will hate me forever.

This feat of acrobatic genius meant that every day they were able to descend for something to eat, and then retreat before they were detected. This kept them safe for a few weeks until they were a lot bigger and a lot hungrier. Unfortunately, the food that was being delivered was only food for one, because as far as the humans were concerned, there was only one chicken in the shed. Each of them was only getting a third of the food they needed and that didn't bode well for the future. They either needed more food, or a way out.

Betty stared at Brian. Brian stared at Betty. Brain thought as hard as he could and Betty thought just as hard. There was nothing. No plan, no procedure, no daring escapade that might get them out of their predicament. They were resigned to their fate, until Alectryon was once again looking in their direction, and fate dealt them a helping hand/foot/wing.

It was pretty windy outside. It was raining hard. There were various things flying around the garden and crashing into each other. A bucket smashed the greenhouse, a bike got blown into the pond, the compost bin was upended and several tiles fell off the roof of the house. The stroke of luck for Brian and Betty was the piece of chimney which landed on the hen house and made a hole in the top.

This would help their mother to escape, but then she was quite happy where she was and would have plenty to eat once they were gone. One brief look into her soul[133] as a heartfelt goodbye and they threw each up the last part of

---

[133] She didn't have much of a soul and she had no idea that they were looking into it.

the wall of their shed and through the hole at the top. They were free.

For the first time in this story, the chicken protagonists - on this occasion - were able to fly. Not because their wings were bigger, or their bodies more lithe. Not because of some weird twist of genetics or cross-breeding. Simply because it was incredibly windy.

Brian held on to Betty's foot, they spread their piddly wings as wide as they were able, and let the wind take them to wherever they were destined to go. It was a fairly short journey which took them to the artificial island in the middle of a pond in a local country park. They were 'caught' by a tree and managed to anchor themselves on a branch and weather the remainder of the storm together.

In the calm after the storm, our brother and sister team were able to survey their surroundings. Whilst they had become used to someone throwing food in for them every day, they quickly discovered that using their faces to find worms was entirely instinctive. The parts of them that were avian were overjoyed at every wriggling morsel that they tugged from the ground. The parts of them that were human were repulsed with every squishy little 'face'. They were simultaneously gurgling with anticipation and gagging with revulsion.

There were a few trees on the island, some lighting boxes, some ducks and a whole host of geese. The ducks scarpered whenever Brian or Betty got anywhere near them, but the geese were different. They were evil. They seemed to have a pack mentality and herded the chickens by surrounding them. The geese were massive compared to our plucky bantams, and being surrounded by them was intensely intimidating. Betty stared at Brian. Brian stared at Betty. Their connection was made; they linked wings and started spinning. Together they were a mass of spinning, squawking feathers which must have looked like industrial machinery to the geese, who immediately dispersed. Picture the scene; a whirling dervish of doom, making unlikely noises and spinning uncontrollably. It's not a surprise that the geese saw fit to scarper.

Dizzy and nauseous, they collapsed to the floor and waited for the world to stop moving[134]. They ate worms. They looked at the water. They pecked at the trees a bit. A few hours later, they discovered something that the geese had up their proverbial sleeves which they were unable to counter.

The geese could fly.

One beautiful white goose came in from the sky, folded its wings slightly to speed itself up and dive-bombed Betty. It didn't have claws to pick her up with but it dealt her enough force to knock her into the water. Brian started panicking because he had no idea whether chickens could swim. A few minutes later, a squelchy Betty dragged herself up onto the bank and filled in the gaps in his knowledge; chickens are not exactly equipped with paddling equipment, but they float well and can largely direct themselves. They don't have waterproof feathers though, so hyperthermia replaced drowning and geese as the most relevant threat to life.

---

[134] It didn't actually stop moving. If it had then this would be a very different book about the end of the world and the end of gravity as we know it. It just moved slowly, although it didn't really do that either.

They adopted their climbing trick and threw each up one of the bushier trees and into the crook of two large branches. Brian plucked leaves from the tree and built them up around Betty until her shivering stopped, and they spent the night in an indelicately woven nest. Brian dreamt of rafts.

In the morning, Brian set out to find as many twigs as he could, and together they wove them in and out of each other until they had something that might float. Although chickens **can** swim, they are a long way from 'Olympic' standard; swimming less than a metre was almost too much for Betty and then of course there was the issue of the cold. Their raft looked awful but seemed fairly solid. Using a branch each as a poorly designed paddle, they painstakingly splashed their way across the pond.

"Mummy! Chicken on a boat!"

"Yes dear…"

"Over there…"

"That's lovely dear…"

"Splashy splashy!"

"Of course…"

A small child strapped into a pushchair was pointing enthusiastically at Betty and Brian as they edged across the pond. Its mum had parked the child with half a loaf of stale bread to feed the ducks with, and was on the phone to a friend, largely ignoring the child.

"Can I have a chicken?"

"Maybe for Christmas sweetheart…"

"I love chickens."

Somewhere in amongst that, the mother probably thought that the child had confused ducks and chickens. At no point did she turn around to look, but her responses would eventually lead to the mother being forced to buy a few chickens and a henhouse. Fifteen years later, that same child would be the owner of some of the most successful fighting cocks that Britain had ever seen, and the child would be heading for several years in prison.

At this stage, though, he was still a cute toddler who liked birds, and whose mother didn't pay him enough attention.

Meanwhile, Betty and Brian made it to the other side of the pond and scuttled into the bushes that lined the path by the pond. By the time the mother turned around, there were just ducks and encroaching geese. This was the beginning of almost a year of pester-power, culminating in inevitable chicken ownership. She didn't know what she was letting herself in for.

Our chickens were free.

Off they clucked, into the unknown. For an unspecified length of time, this was their life. They became 90% chicken, using their 10% human guile to evade capture and find safe places to sleep. They ate worms, hid, slept, dug holes with their feet and ate more worms. Occasionally they gorged themselves on bird seed in strangers' gardens. By way of thanks, Betty laid her eggs in those same gardens wherever possible.

Whilst to Betty this was a gesture of goodwill, to most ordinary people it is pretty freaky to find a clutch of unexplained chicken eggs in their garden. Very few people would eat them if they didn't know where they came from, and in some cases there were other outcomes for those eggs. She laid some on a back doorstep and you can imagine what happened to them. She laid some others in a laundry basket full of clean laundry; one very unfortunate lady got more than she bargained for when she put her bra on before she was fully awake. Some eggs were laid in shoes, which again were short-lived. Most were just thrown away. It is a blessing that Betty never saw the fate of her labours; she was able to walk away thinking she had Done a Good Thing.

When October came around and the trees started to turn, things started looking a bit less rosy. They couldn't roost in trees with no leaves for cover, the ground was starting to freeze and they could no longer penetrate it to find food. It was also really cold, and cuddling together just wasn't enough.

One sunny afternoon, Betty spotted a doughnut in a paper bag under a pushchair. Whilst the chauffeur of the pushchair looked like he was otherwise engaged, she jumped into the paper bag to liberate the doughnut, becoming increasingly entangled as she shredded the bag with her wriggling. With dazzlingly bad timing, a bus arrived and the pushchair was loaded up before Betty even realised she was moving. Brian watched in horror as his whole world was driven away on a Number 76 bus.

Brian didn't know what to do. He tried chasing the bus for about 20 metres, but was inexplicably unable to keep up. He watched it disappear off into the distance, around a roundabout and away. A part of Brian was on that bus too and he knew from that moment that he would spend the rest of his life looking for his beloved sister.

That night, he slept in a hedgehog house (sans hedgehog) with some straw, and planned his next move.

The word 'planned' is perhaps an overstatement. What actually happened is that he repeated "Must find Betty" hundreds of times until he went to sleep. Not exactly a plan, but an end goal at least.

The following morning, Brian did something he had never done before, which was to crow[135] when the sun came up. He Doodle-do'ed[136] to his heart's content, until the owner of the garden he was in thrust open the curtains in her birthday suit and flashed at the world, struggling to believe what her ears were telling her. They weren't; it really was a chicken on the shed roof. She threw a slipper in the general direction of the shed and was impressed at the distance but disappointed by the aim.

Brian began a 360° turn on the shed roof until something deep in his soul told him to stop. The house owner watched what looked like a live weathervane in awe, turned to call for her partner to have a look, and then booked a counselling session when she turned back to see that There Was No Chicken.

---

[135] Why do cockerels crow? Surely crows should crow? Does that mean crows cock?

[136] I know this is bad grammar, but 'doodle-dood' seemed even more wrong.

Brian was not wasting any time. With steely determination, he began a marathon in the direction in which he felt he was being pulled with animal magnetism[137]. Nothing was going to stop him, and no shits were given about anything that got in his way. He went through a greenhouse[138] and out through a (freshly broken) pane of glass at the other end. He went through a dense hawthorn hedge and left a lot of his feathers behind. He went through a pond, by bouncing across a convenient fountain pump in the middle. He ran through a bonfire and singed a tail feather. He crossed several roads in stages, like a character in a well known computer game (but with more convincing sound effects).

Why did the chicken cross the road(s)? To find his sister, obviously.

There were occasionally distractions - mainly food and sleep-related - but the general pattern was to run until he couldn't. There were some obstacles that were insurmountable; a wall higher than a metre was impossible, although he deserved top marks for trying, despite the damage he repeatedly did to his face. There was a row of houses which he was unable to go over or under[139], and there was one fence whose gaps weren't quite big enough for a Brian. It took three stuck heads and a near garrotting for him to work that out.

---

[137] This isn't really what 'animal magnetism' means. Just saying.

[138] It would have been much easier to go around, but this was a Chicken on a Mission.

[139] Some members of the community were thoroughly discombobulated by the array of small holes being dug along the perimeter of their houses. Most put it down to foxes, which seem to be blamed for a lot.

The biggest issue was a river which meant a long diversion to find a bridge, leading on to the discovery that trains move a lot faster than cars. Brian had thought that the long, quiet, metal rails looked like an excellent transport option. When the 5.26 commuter service from Birmingham came hurtling up behind him, he very quickly learned why $V = D/T$[140] is an important concept in life. Apparently, Brian was Alectryon's favourite chicken and he was just short enough to be missed by the train and just light enough to avoid getting sucked onto the tracks. His battered tail did get caught in the coupling device that held the carriages together, and he found himself clinging on to a connecting rod for dear life while the train barrelled off in exactly the direction that Brian was already heading in.

At the next station, Brian disembarked from his entanglement in the train like a seasoned commuter and carried on running, entirely unaware of how close he'd been to becoming a chicken pancake.

Brian's Twin Radar was powerful and was dragging him down a quiet road that lead away from the train station. There were no cars (which was a blessing) and no people (also a blessing). The road was smooth underfoot and the sun was warm on his face. His internal homing device was beeping furiously and he couldn't wait to see his beloved sister.

At the end of the road there was a detached family home with a beautiful lawn and storybook flowers around the door. Brian **knew** that Betty was there somewhere - he just didn't know how to get to her. There was a fence, and it was

---

[140] Velocity (speed in a specific direction) is calculated by dividing displacement by time. I'm sure you knew that already, as you were doubtless an outstanding Physics student at school…

higher than the walls that he already knew he couldn't climb. There was a gate, and it was closed. With all entrances barred, Brian sat down and engaged every brain cell that wasn't thinking of worms. In his head, he built a catapult device which propelled him into the garden and then rescued Betty by picking the lock on the gate with his beak. In practice, he just sat there until a car came, and ran in behind it; much less heroic but equally effective.

Around the side of the house and into the back garden, and there she was. The sun glinted on her feathers and when Brian's eyes met Betty's, she squawked with glee. This was a weirdly inappropriate moment, where the line between 'sister' and 'object of endless passion' became momentarily blurred. She came towards him, and he realised there were bars between them; she was encased in a chicken mansion. It was big and beautiful and - sadly - sturdy. No amount of pecking opened the door and no amount of shoving shifted it.

The chicken wire was buried deep into the ground to make it fox-proof (and Brian-proof), and the roof was very firmly attached. The holes in the wire were barely big enough for a chicken's head[141] and there were no windows. It was bolted shut, at a height conveniently above that which either chicken could realistically reach. There was a lot of staring, wing flapping and nondescript jumping but no conclusions were made or shared.

---

[141] Both siblings tried. Both siblings got stuck for an embarrassing amount of time. One spun all the way around against the wire and the other got one foot stuck in an effort to get free. Both failed. Neither learned anything at all from the experience.

It was a neatly slatted shed with each slat of wood overlapping the other slightly to keep the weather out. Brian made some impressively gymnastic manoeuvres, which culminated in him facing the ground with the claws on both feet tucked underneath one of the slats, so that he could grip it and pull it upwards and backwards if he used all of his strength. The slat moved, but not enough that he might have been able to tear it off with brute force. It gave him hope though; all he needed was the right tools and a bit of additional brainpower.

He wasn't strong enough for a crowbar or a hammer, but could just about manage a decent-sized screwdriver. He was a relatively small fowl, and found that he could squeeze under the garage door, giving him access to a full arsenal of tools, most of which he couldn't even identify. There were power tools that would have solved all of his problems at once, but the logistics of using and operating them put them firmly in the "Don't waste your time" category. Eventually, he found two flat-headed screwdrivers and took them outside, one at a time. He poked one through the bars to Betty and kept one for himself. Betty chose a slat that was fairly close the ground, wedged the screwdriver in[142]. She then fluttered up to perch on it so that it moved enough that Brian could see it from the outside and put his own tool into the corresponding hole[143], get underneath it, and push at the same time as Betty. On the count of three[144], they both put all of their energy into breaking in/out of a single slat. After

---

[142] I'm not going to imagine how she might have done this and I think the least unlikely option is that she held it in one of her feet. Let's go with that.

[143] Tool. Hole. <snigger>

[144] It was more "Cluck, **cluck CLUUUUCK**" than "One, two three" but the end result was the same.

several attempts, there was a **pop** and a nail flew out. One more set of heaving, and another nail flew out.

This was an excellent start; just three more slats to go and there would be a chicken-sized gap to play with.

Slat number two was straightforward and created a hole big enough for a head and neck, but not a body. Slat number 3 was a challenge because Brian couldn't reach the gap that he needed to jam his screwdriver into. After a succession of items were dragged over to create a makeshift set of steps, and Brian recognised that his balance was awful, then rearranged his scaffolding accordingly, he was ready to make the final steps to his secure sister's freedom.

Time was of the essence; Brian heard a car pulling up onto the drive so there would soon be witnesses to the escape of the century. They pushed, pulled, grunted, squawked and jumped up and down until they'd both shat themselves[145] several times and there were more loose feathers than anyone was comfortable with. The slat squeaked, bent and eventually tumbled to the floor. Betty was free. Brian was the hero. Everything was right in the world.

Their exertions had kept them so busy that they hadn't noticed what was happening above them. Through a wonderful shade of grey-purple, the sky had turned dark grey because the clouds were suddenly a thick fleece overhead, blocking most of the sun and warning of imminent crises. As the two fowl did the closest thing possible to an embrace, the first few hailstones came down first gradually, and then ferociously.

---

[145] It probably only counts as shitting oneself, if one is wearing clothes, otherwise it's probably just shitting.

If you've ever been hit in the face by a hailstone, you'll know it can hurt. If those hailstones are coming thick and fast, the size of a marble, and you're a chicken then it's more than just a bit of hurting. Brian and Betty did exactly what any sentient chicken would do, and took cover in the shed they had just vacated, because it was the closest offer of cover that there was. It felt like they were inside a colossal drum kit and there was a family of twelve hammering away on the roof above them. It was invigorating and frightening and - ultimately - a very brief experience.

A cursory flick through a Geography textbook will tell you some interesting things about hailstorms:

- They come from tall cumulonimbus clouds.
- They can travel at up to 68mph.
- Jericho in Kenya has more hail than anywhere else on Earth.
- The heaviest hailstone in history weighed just over 1kg, and the biggest was almost 18cm across.
- Hailstorms generally come in combination with thunder and lightning.

It was this last point which was the most significant as far as Betty and Brian were concerned. Just moments after they found shelter, 300,000,000 volts leapt out of the heavens, like Alectryon had finally decided these two feathered felons weren't worth his time, and farted in their general direction.

300,000,000 volts is a lot of volts. Betty and Brian's hearty reunification culminated in two fairly small portions of roast chicken, and that was that.

Robin

Robin had nothing in his stomach, otherwise he would have immediately shared it on his arrival in the world. He was born retching, thanks to the not-so-gentle swaying motion of his 'home'. He retched into the straw and wriggled a bit until he was upright, and then the swaying sent him right back to the ground. He looked around him, which offered no clues at all, because it was dark. He spread his wings out to feel around him but that didn't help either because he wings were only 2cm across.

So. He was lying on straw, in the dark, moving slightly, and desperate to be sick; not the best first day for a newborn chick.

Day 2: Daylight edged across the floor and revealed a cage, nine other very subdued chickens and a lot of straw. And an eggshell. This time he wanted to eat more than he wanted to spew, and crept to his unsteady feet. He found something that was probably food, ate it, and then spewed[146]. He wobbled over to the edge of the cage, which was pressed against a round window. Through the window he could see miles and miles of wavy stuff, which he would later describe as sea.

Day 3: Robin was getting the hang of walking and identifying the difference between food and chicken shit. He knew every inch of the $50cm^2$ that he was able to call home, and could identify every member of his flock by scent and chirrup. He was still tiny but he had found his voice and his feet and was making the most of both of them until the day that everything stopped.

---

[146] Sometimes, small brown pellets are **not** food…

There was a massive metallic BANG, and some lurching. This was followed by screaming in other parts of the ship, some loud splashing and some other noises that Robin could not identify. Another big lurch and the cage slid off whatever it was on, fell to the ground, and smashed. Some of the other feathered beauties were too slow and too stupid to get out in one piece, but tiny Robin missed all of the debris and claws and squishing, and kept hopping until he was away from anything that might flatten him. He leapt up the steps leading out of the bowels of the boat and found himself on the deck, sliding towards the edge of a rapidly lilting boat. As he plummeted off the edge and into the Atlantic, he took the precaution of grabbing something with a flailing foot before splashing into the ocean.

What he had grabbed was the hand luggage of an artist who had been planning to paint a tropical island paradise. It was a small plastic wheelie case with a zip all the way around the edge; the only permeable part of the case. As a result, as long as the zip stayed above below the water, it didn't fill up and made a remarkably effective raft. This was the first time Robin had seen or touched water, and he certainly didn't understand the concept of paddling or tides or the thermo-saline circulation system[147]. So he sat on the case and waited for something to happen.

Day 4: He sat on the case some more, and continued to wait.

Day 5: He lay on the case because he was too hot and tired and hungry to stand on it.

---

[147] This is the combination of heat and salt content which makes bits of the sea move from one place to the other.

Day 6: This day essentially didn't happen because Robin was clinging onto life with the thinnest of threads, and was unconscious.

Day 7: Robin was dragged from the brink of death by a seagull who thought he was dead. He squeaked at the seagull in what he thought was an aggressive fashion, but the seagull simply wasn't used to its food talking and flew away to contemplate its life choices. Robin stood up and saw his saviour of a suitcase on the sand next to him, still closed and apparently unscathed.

At that moment, several bolder seagulls descended on the suitcase and between them they picked it up and strained as they dragged it skyward and then dropped it again when our tiny Robin[148] launched himself at them, chirping as loudly as his 1cm lungs would allow. They were taken by surprise, and this manifested itself in them opening their beaks to say the gull equivalent of "Oooooh", which meant dropping the case, from about 7m up in the air.

7m turned out to be the absolute limit of the hinge on a suitcase, and it burst open on the beach, ripping the zip and sharing its contents with the world. After a brief swoop from a couple of hopeful flappers, the scavengers decided that there was nothing edible in the haul. Robin was able to investigate without interruption, and discovered half a cheese sandwich (hidden under some trousers), some underwear, a bag of tiny jelly sweets, a phone charger (but no phone), and a lot of paint.

He ate as much of the sandwich as he could (which wasn't much, given his tiny frame) and rested under the shade of

---

[148] Who - confusingly - was **not** a Robin

some lacy knickers until he felt ready to tackle the world, which turned out to be tomorrow.

Day 8: It was time for Robin to - metaphorically - spread his wings. He clambered out of the knickers, mountaineered out of the case and made his way up towards the trees that lined the beach. It was a long way on very short legs, but when it started to rain, Robin was glad of the shelter offered by the trees, and the water that he was able to glean from droplets on giant leaves. There were noises and smells that he'd never come across before[149] but it was exciting and he couldn't get enough of it. As he sat and watched the world go by, a cacophony of colour appeared from behind him and started stripping the trees above bare of whatever fruit they yielded. It was fascinating and beautiful and Robin couldn't take his eyes off them. They worked as a team, staying close together and apparently communicating with each other at every stage of their journey. Then they stopped, the lights went out[150] and everyone concerned went to sleep.

Day 9: The birds were gone when Robin woke up, and he explored further into the forest to see what else he could find. There were mushrooms that were bouncy (and mushrooms that exploded when he jumped on them). There were ants which carried giant chunks of undergrowth around with them, and ants which surrounded Robin like he was their next proper meal. Fortunately, even a baby chicken can outrun an ant. There were flowers as big as Robin and trees so big that he couldn't see their crowns.

---

[149] If we think about it, almost **all** noises and smells were new to him; his life experience was very limited and he was born in a cage.

[150] Translation: the sun went down

Then there was the Thing With Teeth[151]. It looked at Robin, sniffed him, then snorted through its nostrils in what was either an angry or an inquisitive way - Robin wasn't sure. They eyeballed each other, which was an interesting experience because the Thing With Teeth had eyeballs bigger than Robin's head. He could smell its breath, which was a less than pleasant experience. He could see the remnants of its last meal[152] under its chin. It came closer, sniffed harder, and then picked Robin up - remarkably gently - and left him dangling, briefly.

What came next was both terrifying and exhilarating, with a side order of perplexing. The Thing With Teeth tossed Robin up into the air like a badly misshapen ping pong ball, then batted him to the floor with its paw, claws sheathed. He was then scooped up again, and briefly juggled between two paws, while The Thing stood unsteadily on its back feet for an instant before dropping to the ground again. This was repeated several times until Robin had what he thought was an opportunity to escape, and he took it.

Just as he got up to full speed, a giant paw surrounded him, with claws out like prison bars trapping him, but didn't go through him. The paw slowly lifted up and he gazed into the eyes of The Thing, which seemed almost full of glee[153].

---

[151] It also had sleek fur, pointy ears, whiskers and an enthusiastically swooshing tail, but it was only the teeth that Robin was interested in.

[152] Impossible to identify precisely, but whatever it was, it had red blood. A really helpful piece of information when engaging in amateur taxonomy.

[153] In the absence of eyebrows, it's fairly difficult to ascertain the emotional journey of any kind of cat, but Robin was sure that this one was smiling.

He was released. He ran. He was trapped again. Once again, those wild eyes peered in at him, and then let him go.

Sometimes he was allowed to go 30cm, sometimes it was further. Sometimes there were two paws, and sometimes there was one, but he zigzagged along the forest floor like a chick possessed. Then there was a moment of genius; instead of running forward, he ran backwards, and The Thing tried (in vain) to pounce backwards under itself, grabbing its own tail. Robin was still very young, and could not help but laugh, pointing one fluffy wing at The Thing as it disentangled itself. He miscalculated the speed with which The Thing would regain its composure, and thus missed his opportunity to run.

The paw - squish - escape - paw - squish - escape cycle carried on until The Thing tired, whereupon there was a pause at the 'squish' stage. Robin had an instant to look out through the gaps between its fingers[154] and spotted a hole in the undergrowth; he just needed to get there.

The Thing carried on with its game, and Robin edged closer to what he hoped would be his best hope. When the moment came, he threw himself into the hole he'd spotted, not caring what might be inside. Whatever it was, it was much smaller than The Thing and therefore much less scarier and much less immediate.

Or so he thought.

Before he'd even remembered how to breathe properly, eight beady eyes shone out at him and an equivalent number of hairy legs, walking in an unfeasibly robotic way

---

[154] They're technically toes, but it was using its paws more like hands than feet, so 'fingers' seemed more appropriate.

came towards him. He didn't know what it was, but it wasn't screaming "friend" at him.

He waited, unable to move. Behind him was The Thing and in front of him was The Smaller Thing. Both seemed to lead to the same conclusion, which did not seem to involve seeing Day 10.

Day 10: Robin was overjoyed to be wrong. The end of the previous day did not exist in the recesses of his memory, but he now found himself wrapped tightly[155] and underground, staring once again at The Smaller Thing, which had its head cocked on one side like an excited puppy. A small shaft of light squeezed in through a long entrance hole. At this point, Robin wasn't sure whether he was a companion or an appetiser.

The Smaller Thing scuttled around its cocoon, admiring it from every angle. It was used to encapsulating grasshoppers and similarly sized bugs; Robin was something of an unexpected trophy and The Smaller Thing wasn't really sure where to start. It poked Robin with its furry little legs, which sent shivers down his spine; the poking was more menacing than massage and day 10 suddenly seemed like just a stay of execution. As The Smaller Thing scuttled excitedly around several solid meals, it dislodged dust from the floor of its lair until the 'room' was thick with debris.

---

[155] Ironically, he was trussed up like a chicken…

Robin sneezed[156]. The sneeze made his body convulse slightly, and in that instant he saw a chink of hope. He breathed in as much and as fast as he could, until another sneeze erupted. He convulsed again, every muscle in his body flexing at once for the tiniest instant. The Smaller Thing seemed taken aback, as though each sneeze was a burst of black magic that could make his legs curl up and shrivel. It backed away slightly, scared. The sneezing carried on until Robin was starting to feel dizzy but it was working. With every sneeze, his feet[157] rubbed against the cocoon, slowly carving out an exit strategy. The more sneezing there was, the bigger the hole in the cocoon got, until Robin could squeeze out and once again stood on his own two feet.

This was a new experience for The Smaller Thing. It wasn't used to its dinner fighting back and/or exploding, and it was cowering in a corner[158], trying to cover some of its eyes with some of its legs. This was an impressive, but ultimately unsuccessful attempt to hide from what it was certain had been sent to kill it. For maximum effect, Robin aimed one last sneeze at The Smaller Thing, which coiled in on itself in response. Robin trotted back out into the sunshine, head held high, and found somewhere safe[159] to hide.

---

[156] If you have ever heard a bird sneeze, you will know that it is one of the most ridiculous sounds in the world. Cats and dogs sneeze, and they look/sound cute with a little shake of the head and a brief look of total confusion. Chickens just look incredibly stupid and very confused.

[157] If you've ever been scratched by a chicken (or seen a chicken after a fight), you'll know quite how sharp their feet are.

[158] This was a figurative corner. The burrow was round, and circles have no corners.

[159] Or at least saf**er** - this was a *relative* concept in the circumstances.

Day 11: This time, our rapidly growing floof woke up under a leaf, with precisely zero eyes staring at him and absolutely no large mammals juggling with him. This was a good start to the day, fortified with the view above him; those birds he had seen before were once again perched in the trees above. They were resplendent in red, blue, yellow and green[160], with hooked beaks that they used to strip and eat every ounce of fruit in each tree as though it were bread dough[161]. They fluttered effortlessly from branch to branch, and spoke to each other with squawks and chirping that sounded like opera to Robin[162]. There was nothing he wanted more than to be with them; so high up, so graceful and so free. He clambered up into a bush, spread his wings and thrust himself into the air, hoping he would glide like them.

He didn't.

That night, he dreamed of fruit, flying, birdsong and gravity.

Day 12: Robin was a Chicken on a Mission. He was bright enough to have worked out that his wings and body did not entirely match. He couldn't see a future where he was sleek

---

[160] Contrary to popular belief, chickens are not colourblind. They can actually see colour better than we can, although I can't imagine what they need it for! Worms only come in one colour, and traffic lights are rarely an issue encountered in chickenhood.

[161] At the 'editing' stage of writing this ridiculous tome, I am unable to work out what I was thinking when I used 'like bread dough' as a simile. I'm certain that it made sense when I wrote it, so I thought I'd leave it in just in case a reader somewhere might understand my train of thought better than I seem to. Send me a postcard/email/carrier pigeon if you can work out what the hell I meant.

[162] Clearly Robin was more cultured than me. I hate opera.

and aerodynamic, but he did wonder whether he could do anything to make his wings more than just ornamental.

He spent the rest of the day adorning his wings with a succession of items which he hoped might give him flight. He gathered feathers that had fallen from the parrots in the trees. Fail. He tried an assortment of leaves of different shapes and sizes. Messy fail. He tried twigs, fanned out, like a… fan. Heavy fail. He tried pieces of bark, stripped from the trees. Dusty fail. He tried some flower petals. Beautiful fail. Every time, he took himself to a high point, and took his chances. Every time he fell, and every time he bounced. After the 9th attempt, he was losing patience and he was starting to lose feathers.

In a final act of desperation, he hunted for all of his **own** feathers (some left his teensie rump with every plummet), and carefully re-engineered them into his wings. Whilst this didn't help him to fly, it did at least help him to glide to the ground in a slightly more controlled way, which was progress.

One of the parrots glode[163] to a perch just above Robin's head, and watched him for a while. It made a pleasant change to be watched by something that didn't look like it wanted to kill him, and Robin felt comfortable with the fluttering rainbow next to him. It got progressively closer, until it was right next to him, watching him intently.

Then it was gone, and Robin was left to his own devices, perfecting the art of not crashing.

---

[163] 'Glode' is not a word, but then I don't think 'glided' is either. I could look it up, but whatever the dictionary says, they both sound like made up words.

A short time later, the parrot returned, with an assortment of feathers in its mouth. He stretched his wings and gestured Robin to do the same, his paltry[164] flying apparatus puny by comparison. Far more gently than Robin could ever have anticipated, the parrot carefully inserted one feather after the other into the assortment of feathers that were already there. The scarlet ones hardly blended in to his dull brown body, but they were woven in such a fashion that they almost looked like they belonged. Together, they practised[165] jumping out of trees until Robin was battered and bruised, but also in the general direction of successful flying/gliding.

Robin had a friend, and Robin could (almost) fly.

Day 13: Waking up like a film star on the day of an awards ceremony in which they had several nominations, Robin stretched his wings, his feet and his neck, out into the warming morning sun. He admired his 'new' wings and listened to the sounds of the forest around him. He was so excited that he could burst, as he scrabbled around for some fruity leftovers or wriggly breakfast nuggets.

His little friend found him and together, they made it to the top of a tree. The parrot flew, while Robin flapped, clawed and bit his way to the top, in the least graceful way possible. There, they were quickly surrounded by the parrot's friends, family and other known associates, who were keen to investigate their new charge.

---

[164] Paltry or poultry? Couldn't resist...

[165] One day I'll work out the difference between 'practised' and 'practiced'. Today is not that day.

They came, they saw, and then they attacked. Robin clattered down through the undergrowth like a loaf of bread that was slightly undercooked[166], and came to rest several billion miles below[167]. His little friend followed him down - albeit in a rather more controlled way than previous attempts - and sat with him until he could breath and cluck properly again. At this point, the parrot gestured towards his own feathers, and then back towards Robin's. Robin was not firing on all cylinders at this point and it took him a while to work out that the parrot was pointing out that Robin was considerably less beautiful than the rest of the flock. There was no beating about the bush; Robin was brown and frankly he would never fit in.

Day 14: Day 13 had not been a resounding success, but Robin remained undeterred. He retraced his steps back to the beach that he'd first arrived on, and eventually found his suitcase washed up a little further along the shore. In it, unscathed, were several tubes of acrylic paint. Robin dragged them out, one at a time, and laid them on the inside of the suitcase top. He unscrewed each lid through some miracle of pecking, jumping and angry flapping, then jumped with his full force (which wasn't much) on each tube until a colourful snake escaped from within. He paid particular attention to the red tube, and gave it an extra 'squeeze'[168].

---

[166] Dense, solid, but ultimately bouncy.

[167] Obviously it wasn't several billion miles, but when you're falling from a height, things slow down. To Robin, it felt like hours. He actually only fell about 20m, but that's a long way when you can't fly.

[168] 'Squeeze' is a less than accurate description of what he was doing. If you squeezed a person like he was 'squeezing' the tubes of paint, you'd be in a special jacket with arms that tie up at the back very quickly.

The next part was a lot of fun. He rolled around in the paint like a pig rolling around in shit (but more fragrant). He squidged it into, under and around every feather until even his skin was kaleidoscopic. He emerged from the suitcase a totally different bird, and waddled along the sand, absorbing sand and leaving paint in equal measure. He stood for a moment on a warm rock, to admire himself in the sunlight before stepping into the forest. This was his undoing. Acrylic paint is essentially made out of plastic, and dried paint can melt when heated. At this point, Robin was stuck to a rock, and the vultures[169] had spotted him already.

He heaved. He wriggled. He tried hopping, with negligible results. He made "Oomph" noises, which made him feel like he was putting some serious effort in but made no real difference to his predicament. In fact, the ooomphing simply drew attention to him, which brought The Thing padding back towards him. The Thing was apparently feeling less playful today; with what passed for a 'dirty look', it took a massive swipe at Robin, which stripped him from his rock and sent him sprawling back onto the sand, where he rolled a few times before stopping. By this point, 96% of the beach[170] was stuck to his feathers. He looked on in terror, unable to move (mainly because every part of him was welded together) as The Thing softly advanced, drooling slightly and twitching on one side of its face. Robin didn't know what praying was, but if he had, he would be doing it. Frantically.

---

[169] They were technically seagulls, but they were behaving like vultures.

[170] Obviously it wasn't 96%. Technically it was probably about 0.000000000000000000000002%.

The Thing was in his face in one dainty step, its breath so warm that it fogged up Robin's eyeballs. Under normal circumstances, he would have blinked. Unfortunately, there was a thin layer of 'empire green' along the bottom of both eyelids, so he couldn't close them. A huge and remarkably pink tongue flopped out, and licked him from top to bottom, then made whatever noise it makes when you try and spit your own tongue out.

When a child eats a lollipop that's unnaturally blue, its tongue changes colour, and it briefly looks like an alien lifeform[171]. This is what happened to The Thing, whose tongue was a combination of 'Indian Red' and 'Yellow brick road', with a thin dusting of sand. Its wrath was spent on the world in general and Robin was spared.

Well… he **thought** he was spared. His immobility made him perfect fodder for the seagulls (again), and he'd been picked from the sand before he could even blink[172]. Seagulls are stronger than you might think, and small chickens are correspondingly lighter than you might think. In fact, Robin was actually heavier than the seagull thought, and it failed to get quite the height it had expected before several other seagulls decided that it was time to share, and each grabbed a limb. He was being 'shared' by four different gulls, who had a hold of both feet and both wings… but none of them had thought to get control of his head and his pointy little beak.

---

[171] There is a school of thought that thinks children **always** look like alien lifeforms. We'll park that thought there.

[172] This was actually quite a long time, given the paint/eye situation.

He released one leg, then one wing, so he was hanging entirely on one side. One more energetic peck, and he tumbled back towards the canopy below, where 12 different trees broke his fall. By the time he made it to ground zero, the majority of the sand had been knocked off and he was just a fraudulent parrot again, resemblant in full technicolour.

As he gradually grained whatever remnants of dignity he had left, his friend returned from the tangled mass above and cocked his head in what Robin assumed was a 'confused' way. He smelt like a Robin[173], he had the eyes and beak of a Robin, but he was a sticky meld of red, green and blue. Robin clucked and his friend realised that it was him after all and did a little dance on his branch.

They did some practice 'flights', where Robin tested out his sticky (but surprisingly sturdy) wings by scrambling to the top of something high and taking his chances, with mixed reviews. Some were a horrific failure, some horrendous failure and the occasional catastrophic failure, none of which could be described as flying, even if viewed from a very long way away, through squinted eyes, in the dark. On the final 'flight', Robin seemed to be in more trouble than previously, and his friend felt the need to rescue him before he hit the tree that was inconveniently in his flightpath. His friend, who we'll call Polly[174], hovered up underneath him and took his weight, in time to steer him away from impending doom. With rather more effort than normal and a small amount of support from Robin's largely useless wings,

---

[173] Just in name; he wasn't actually a robin, just a chicken called Robin. He didn't look like a Robin that you might get on Christmas cards, because they aren't green. I perhaps could have chosen a less confusing name.

[174] ...mainly because I feel I may as well continue with the pattern of terrible naming practices.

they actually got some height. Not a lot of height, but enough to avoid crashing towards certain death.

Tandem flight was apparently the way forward, so they practiced a bit from various heights of vegetation, until they had perfected[175] launch, general movement and landing. Later that evening, as the sun was setting, the rest of the flock arrived and surrounded our daring duo. If he kept his head down and tucked his feet in, he blended in - sort of. They didn't seem to notice him at all, and he kept his beak firmly shut. He roosted happily with his new flock, excited about the prospect of finally hitting the sky[176].

Day 15: The Squawking started as the sun came up and warmed Robin's crisply colourful feathers like all the other 'parrots' They began nibbling at nearby fruit, and he did the same. This was the beginning of the end for Robin. Chickens generally eat grubs, worms and grains. They do not generally eat melons and pomegranates and Robin didn't really know how to deal with fruit, or - more specifically - fruit peel.

He ate as much as was possible[177] whilst his buddies gorged themselves, and then it was time to depart. The others took flight, Polly assumed the position, and Robin fluttered on. They launched. They soared through the air, slowly losing height but generally keeping up with the others. Polly flapped hard, Robin flapped pointlessly but enthusiastically. They made good ground, but Robin was a

---

[175] It wasn't perfect, but it also wasn't fatal, so that was a relative win.

[176] ...rather than the ground...

[177] That was not a lot, because his face was basically the wrong shape.

dense and therefore weighty fowl, who was dragging Polly closer and closer to the canopy. A stray leaf caught one of Polly's feet, and sent her very slightly off balance. It wasn't much, but it was enough to make her wobble. The wobble was enough for Robin to lose all traction and he tumbled off to one side. He would normally have fluttered a bit to avoid reaching terminal velocity, but he was upside down and so he couldn't.

The ground arrived much quicker than he thought it would, and that was the last thought that Robin had.

And there we have it. A chicken which thought it was a person, which thought it was a parrot. Who knew?

Astrid

It was a very loud barn. Chickens are, by nature, chatty creatures. They communicate mainly through emotions; they cackle when they sense danger and they make a noise that's half purr and half cluck when they're contented. A horny rooster croaks and dances, and a chicken will growl when she's not interested. They inform each other when they have found the best bits of food and they sing a sort of lullaby to their children. Astrid found her voice very early on in her life, and - despite fairly consistent use - never lost it.

From the moment she took her first steps, she felt the urge to tell the world about everything she did. Every time the contents of her bowels emerged, she squeaked. When she ate, she gurgled[178] and when she walked, there was a little chirp for every step she made. In a barn with about 3,999 other birds, her tiny rumblings blended in with every other bird when she was small, but it turns out that age and volume are directly proportionate. Whilst all chickens communicate their basic emotions, the range of emotions they experience is smaller than those experienced by people. As Astrid was part person, she had a lot more to get off her chest than most of her barn-mates, none of whom had any idea what she was clucking on about most of the time. This confused and irritated her mother in equal measure, which lead to a lot of pecking incidents for little Astrid. Since her mum was less communicative than her, she was unable to ascertain what she was doing wrong, which lead to her doing what she thought was 'asking lots

---

[178] Children are always taught not to talk with their mouths full, because there's a risk of choking. Astrid never got this particular memo and frankly it's a miracle that her food never killed her.

of questions' but what her mum saw as Just Incredibly Irritating Incessant Noise.

When she was starting to feel the cold as a result of the number of lost feathers from the sanctions meted out by her mother, she moved on to another brood, in the hope that they might be more receptive to her queries about life.

"Hey! Why is the door always closed?"

"Cluck"

"Excuse me - why are we so rubbish at flying?"

"Cluck"

"Er… Where are you in the pecking order?[179]"

"Cluck"

"Can I have some of that please?"

"Cluck"

"Why are you shaking your tail?"

"CLUCK"

…and then she moved on to another 'conversation'. Through this method, she ruffled enough feathers to exclude her from every brood, group and solitary chicken in the barn. She was officially shunned. When she went to eat, they surrounded the feed station so she couldn't get

---

[179] Yes, this is a thing. Astrid was so annoying that she was invariably at the **bottom**.

anywhere near it. Fortunately, chickens like to throw their food around, so there was always plenty left on the floor for her to hoover[180] up. When she tried to snuggle up with another feathered 'friend' for body heat, they poked, prodded and chuntered until she scuttled away. Staying warm was an issue and

Poultry are sociable animals and - like sheep - follow each other around without much concern for making good life decisions. When Astrid found a small gap under the wall of the barn, none of the other birds were interested; they just wanted to carry on doing what all the other chickens were doing, without upsetting the metaphorical apple cart. When she dug out the gap with her feet, the others simply walked around (or over) her. When it was big enough for her to squeeze through, they were in no way bothered, nor did they think it would be sensible to follow. She was free, and the other birds got some respite.

The next few weeks consisted of a lot of wandering around, eating worms and hiding in bushes. Astrid eventually found a landfill site, which had almost limitless supplies of food and plenty of places to hide. The seagulls weren't particularly troublesome, apart from the occasional squirt and one or two dive-bombs. There were rats, but they didn't seem to like the way that Astrid smelled.

Astrid was quite happy pootling around amongst other peoples' throwaway lifestyles. She found all sorts of treasures and gave a running commentary to the world in general as she explored her new world. She'd spent her first months in a barn so everything was new and everything was an adventure. She found three quarters of a kennel, which

---

[180] Other brands of suction-machinery are available.

made a great place to shelter from the rain. She found some teddy[181] clothes and used them to make something like a cave to warm up in. She found all manner of electronics to fiddle with; some bleeped, some whirred, some moved and some had flat batteries. She found a 'brick' mobile phone (because it rang next to her) - she poked it with her beak and a faceless voice said:

"This stuff is amazing - can you get more?"

To which she said:

"I'm not sure - which stuff do you mean?" but of course what the person on the end of the phone heard was "Backaaaaark?" so the line went dead immediately afterwards. What Astrid didn't know was that this was the burner phone for a local drug dealer, whose body lay underneath 76 soft toys[182] just a few metres away. When the phone rang again, it was less positive:

"Don't ignore me you fucking fucker - you're dead if I don't hear from you by midnight..." Although Astrid understood every word, She wasn't sure how to respond, so she poked the red button with her beak, waited a minute, then pecked 9-9-9[183]. When the call handler asked which service she required, she was confused for a minute, and then tapped on the phone screen with her beak

---

[181] We're talking bear, not lingerie...

[182] Some people have a problem with drink, some with drugs and some with tobacco. Other people have a problem with soft toys. It's a much less dangerous habit, but it gets a bit weird when you're a grown adult who has to sit on the floor because the sofa is full of gormless fluffy faces.

[183] The great thing about old brick phones (if you're a chicken) is that they don't need fingers as they're not capacitive.

Tap Tap Tap - Taaaaaap Taaaaaap Taaaaaap - Tap Tap Tap

There was no immediate response while the call handler contemplated what she'd heard. Astrid did it again, and again.

"Are you in danger? Tap once for yes, twice for no…"

Tap

"OK - do you need help?"

Astrid wasn't sure if she did, but she knew she needed something.

Tap

"I'm tracing your call now, and someone will be there urgently."

Then she pressed the red button again, and retreated to her kennel to wait.

Less than hour later, three police cars arrived with their sirens blaring, and started looking around in the rubble. They could find the rough location of the phone but there was an awful lot of crap to sift through and they were heading in the wrong direction. Astrid knew there was no point in making a chicken noise because they'd ignore it. She needed to draw their attention without letting them know what species she was. She found a spatula, and set it up as a catapult[184], with half an apple as the missile. She

---

[184] That's a lie. A catapult is meant to have some kind of string on it, to draw back. This was more like a see-saw, but I don't know what that's called…

jumped on the other end of the spatula and the apple flew a short distance and landed nowhere near the police officers. She needed to up her game as they crept further and further away from the phone and the body that even Astrid wasn't aware of.

She found 2/3 of the slat from a child's bed, a paint can and a clock radio. With this ensemble she succeeded in smashing the radio of PC Nefertari Perret[185]. The next missile was a a mini Spanish dictionary, which sailed past the nose of PC Penn, making him think he was seeing things, but with a strange urge to say "Cojones![186]" loudly. Missile number three needed to be heavy and accurate. It came in the form of the head of a hammer (no handle), which he couldn't budge without jumping onto his catapult from a height.

DCI Sam Rossi regained consciousness two hours later in an ambulance, to the news that his colleagues had found a body and were looking for further evidence. He had absolutely no recollection of anything that had happened that day, but would later receive an award for acting fast on intelligence and surviving an attack in the line of duty. He would never know that it was a chicken who attacked him[187].

Astrid watched the whole thing unfold from a safe distance, and was appropriately smug when she saw how well her cunning plan worked. She shared her smugness with a passing seagull and it shat on her in response. She had

---

[185] This is what happens when you use a random name generator. I'm sorry.

[186] Look it up for yourself.

[187] ...and if he had, he certainly wouldn't have told anyone.

alerted the authorities to a hidden body that even she didn't know about, solving a significant crime with remarkable guile and half a hammer.

Wednesday was bin day, and every Wednesday there was a fresh batch of other peoples' lives to pick through. This particular Wednesday was the day after little Daphne Davies had decided to get rid of the trappings of youth and throw away all of her toys, now that she was a grown-up[188]. Three bin bags full of plastic and bright colours tumbled out of the truck for Astrid's joyful discovery. It was a treasure trove of playthings and every single one was checked over with forensic efficiency. The plastic camera made great noises but didn't take pictures. The jewellery-making set contained small beads which turned out to be inedible. The pump action gun and foam bullets were lethal to seagulls, which was invaluable in maintaining the perimeter of this playground of plastic. There was half a doll with teeth marks around its belly button and its eyes gouged out[189]. It was a life-sized baby doll, and it was terrifying; Astrid turned it over so she didn't have to look at those empty eyes. There was a yellow monster that made a different noise depending on which part of it you poked; a scream from the head, a growl from one foot and a purr from the other. The feet both made a crackling 'this toy is broken' kind of noise. Then there was something conical, with a strap attached to it, and a trigger on the bottom. Astrid squeezed the trigger, but nothing happened, although the trigger jammed, which might explain why it had been thrown away.

---

[188] She was turning 12, but that was 'well old' as far as she was concerned and nobody who is 'well old' plays with toys. Well that's what her friends said, anyway.

[189] Daphne did not like dolls, and fed them to her Labrador whenever possible.

A seagull swooped at that point, and Astrid shot it with a foam bullet.

"Bullseye!"

There was an echo.

How could there be an echo when there was no other sign of life?

"Hello?"

"Hello?"

"Who's there?"

"Who's there?"

The echo was a split second away from the original sound; too fast to be a response because nobody can think that fast.

"What's going on?"

"What's going on?"

This was messing with Astrid's head and she had no answers about what might be going on in her little world. Then there was a click as the trigger on the conical thing unstuck itself.

"Is there anyone there?"

Nothing. As chickens go, Astrid was pretty sharp. It took her a minute to join up all the dots but she did manage to work out that there was a link between the toy and the talking[190]. She took it by its strap and dragged it back to her kennel in case it would be useful later. If she had been an old lady, she would have eventually been on a TV program called something like "Hoarders Unlocked".

She had taken great pleasure in alerting the authorities to the crime scene that she hadn't really been fully aware of, and had developed a taste for it. A landfill site is a great place to dispose of evidence because it would be like searching for a needle in a haystack if you wanted to find something in amongst the discarded fragments of life. For a chicken with a solid brain, no friends and a lot of time on her hands, this was not a problem.

For days, she ripped open bags, opened folded notes and smelled things. The next breakthrough came when she found a t-shirt with a very neat hole in it, and an awful lot of blood. Chickens can't smell a lot, but they can smell blood. She pulled it out of a bag, and found a kitchen knife and several folded notes which turned out to be letters between two people who were definitely not friends. Astrid felt this needed to be shared, so she marked it with a pink hi-vis dog coat, and went off to find a way to let someone know what she'd found, taking her conical shouty thing with her.

Landfill sites are generally built away from people, because nobody wants to live nearby. This one was linked to the world by a network of country lanes frequented by dog walkers and fruity couples looking to steam up their car

---

[190] Just in case you're not following the increasingly thin storyline, the voice-changing toy that Astrid found was translating 'clucking' into English.

windows. Astrid flap-walked[191] down the road for a distance until she saw the rarest of infrastructural relics; a phone box. She ducked her head and tucked underneath the door, where she was immediately overpowered by the stench of piss, because most phone boxes have been repurposed as public toilets. She scuttled out again for a gasp of fresh air and then steeled[192] herself for a second attempt. She bounced her way from side to side up the inside of the phone box, until she could land on the little shelf next to the phone. Once upon a time it would have had a phone book or some loose change on it. Now it had a condom wrapper and a small amount of indistinguishable goop instead. Astrid reached around and knocked the receiver to the ground so that it dangled on its metal cord. She pecked at the '9' button three times[193], then fluttered to the floor and pressed the trigger on her toy.

"Which service do you require?" Came the familiar response.

"Police please"

"Police please" < Brief pause, some clicking sounds, and then some more ringing >

"Can I take your full name and a contact number please?"

---

[191] If you are a chicken and you flap your wings when walking, you go a little faster. This will never be a useful piece of information.

[192] 'To steel' means 'to mentally prepare oneself'. I've been using the phrase 'steel myself' for years and never knew what it meant. Thank-you, internet.

[193] The button was really sticky. It was fortunate that Astrid didn't know why; she would have wanted to bathe in bleach.

"No. There are clothes covered in blood at the rubbish tip. Look for pink hi-vis."

"No. There are clothes covered in blood at the rubbish tip. Look for pink hi-vis."

"Can you rep…" but Astrid couldn't bear the stench any longer and left. There was a 'click' as the trigger unstuck itself. She waddled back to her stomping ground and arrived just before the police, for whom it was clearly another low-crime day as they arrived very fast and with a van full of uniformed officers. From a vantage point on the shoulders of most of a shop mannequin, Astrid watched with fascination as DCI Rossi made it to the crime scene without major injury and recovered the bloody evidence. The surrounding area was subject to a fingertip search and the outcome was a stack of handwritten notes, a knife, a bloody t-shirt and half a bottle of vodka, laced with Rohypnol.

The evidence was instrumental in finding and arresting a disgruntled employee who had attempted to seduce and then stab his boss. Whilst the evidence was conclusive, the defence tried in vain to claim that chicken DNA on the handle of the knife proved that the evidence had been contaminated and that it should therefore be thrown out of court. The judge - for whatever reason - was clear that it was entirely possible that there might have been a chicken at the scene, but did make a point of asking the defence barrister if he was suggesting that the perpetrator was in fact a chicken. The jury stifled a collective laugh, but the barrister did not think it was funny. DCI Rossi had closed another case, and Astrid would only find out about it many months later when she saw pictures of her rubbish tip on the front cover of a passing newspaper on a windy day.

Astrid now took her place in the Hall of Fowl Fame as the most successful chicken detective of all time[194]. She was throughly enjoying herself. The pursuit of justice become her purpose and her pleasure.

Somewhere amongst the flotsam and jetsam of peoples' lives, Astrid found a dog-eared crime novel. It was punctuated by bits of food and - randomly - confetti, but Astrid was pleased to discover that when she looked at the pages of the book, she was able to work out what the words were and make sense of the story. Turning the pages was a struggle but once she got into her stride, she found it immensely pleasurable. Every few pages, some congealed gravy[195] meant that she had to use her powers of deduction to guess some of the words, but the story still made sense. It was a murder mystery, written by someone who seemed to have a PhD in forensic science because the level of detail was extraordinary. There were dog units, clever chemical tests, liberal use of Luminol to find traces of blood and extensive search teams in protective clothing. It filled her head[196] with ideas and when she got to the end[197], she was itching to find some more criminal activity.

Case #3 took a bit more searching. There were no more bloody clothing fragments or murder weapons that she could find in the surface layers of debris, but she did find

---

[194] This was not as impressive as it sounds. Her only competitor was 'Motherclucker', who had exposed the finger of a body buried under her enclosure. She had thought it was a worm and was thoroughly disappointed by the presence of a fingernail.

[195] She hoped it was gravy. It was brown and crisp, so she didn't want to think much further than gravy. Just in case.

[196] This did not take long; her head was very small.

[197] The sister did it. With a roll of toilet paper, in the garage.

some interesting envelopes. Inside one of them there was a fingertip, and a typed note attempting to blackmail the husband of the owner of the finger. It didn't seem to be a complete picture of the situation because it was only half of the correspondence; Astrid needed some more suspicious envelopes. She found several birthday cards (one with money in it), some horrific Valentines' Day poetry and a batch of Christmas cards for a family who had a lot of friends. Somewhere amongst them, she found a handwriting match for the outside of the envelope with the fingertip in it. This seemed like progress and the message inside the card was:

"Maybe this will be the year that you'll say yes? XXX"

So there was a love interest… Was that enough? The phone box was a long way away so she didn't want to make the hike unless she was sure there was enough evidence to get the blue flashing lights out. The letters and cards looked like they'd been there for a while, so it was unlikely to be a life or death situation; Astrid decided to carry on looking. She needed to match the writing on the outside of the Christmas card too and eventually found a diary. It read like something from a teenager's angst-years, and would have featured in the kind of TV programme that airs at 7pm. It was written by a man who seemed to be unhappily married but deeply in love with a driver who worked for a local taxi firm. He therefore took a lot of taxis.

From reading the diary and reading between the lines of some birthday cards that were written in thinly veiled code, Astrid managed to work out some key facts:

- Kris was married to Crystal.
- Crystal was not in the 'Kris' fan club.

- Hendrix drove an electric car, which was really quiet.
- Kris was more serious about Hendrix than Hendrix was about Kris.
- Crystal used Hendrix's taxis too.
- Crystal and Hendrix seemed to be good friends.
- Hendrix did not want anyone to know that he was in any kind of relationship with a man.

Whilst none of this made sense to Astrid, she decided that she had done enough to bring in DCI Rossi. Off she went to the phone, holding her breath while she clambered up to dial the number. She pressed her trigger, got the police to come by telling them there was a blackmail and maybe a kidnapping, and then toddled off again. They came. They searched. They failed to find the makeshift flag that she had left. They searched some more and then left, muttering something about wasting police time. Astrid tried shouting after them but forgot to press the trigger, so all they heard was frantic clucking as they retreated to their cars.

Astrid tried again, this time with a bigger flag and some more high-vis clothing, placed in a circle around the evidence she had uncovered. Again, she called the police, with a little bit more information. She trotted back a little faster than usual, partly so that she was there before the police, and partly because the weather was turning nasty. When she arrived back, the wind had dislodged the high-vis and blown the flag away. Unfortunately for Astrid, DCI Rossi had not forgotten the time he'd wasted last time, and had only brought one other pair of hands with him. They looked (briefly) and didn't find any of the markers that Astrid had left out. She was desperate to keep them there, and switched her trigger on ready for an announcement. She shouted:

"Here! I'm over here! "

"Here! I'm over here!" which had the opposite affect on the situation to that which Astrid expected. It made DCI Rossi think that there was a person in danger, and he immediately called for backup, fearing some kind of imminent collapse. Astrid didn't know that backup was coming, and shouted again:

"What are you doing? I might be dead!"

"What are you doing? I might be dead!" This, of course, made absolutely no sense to DCI Rossi; how could a person be unsure about whether they were dead or not? Generally, dead people don't shout for help, nor are they uncertain of their own breathing status. It was all just a bit weird. Astrid needed to do something to release her stack of paper work to them, so she shouted again.

"I'm obviously not dead. But I think I'm hurt?"

"I'm obviously not dead. But I think I'm hurt?" This seemed like a good way to tempt them in, and DCI Rossi started walking slowly towards the spot where the cards, letters and fingertip were waiting.

Landfill sites are frequented by a lot of wildlife, who visit for the same reasons as Astrid did; lots of food and not many people. Chief among this wildlife are foxes, who love a bit of rotting food. They also have a good sense of smell, and Astrid was a particularly smelly chicken. Just a few metres away, a young vixen had got a whiff of Astrid and was hungry. When she spotted her stalker, Astrid wasn't immediately concerned because she still had one foot on the trigger so she could literally call for help if she needed to.

And she did.

"Hey, I'm…" but at that point she acutely appreciated the drawbacks of pound-store batteries, as her AAs became No-As and her voice was forever silenced. Foxes are much faster than chickens.

When DCI Rossi finally found the evidence he was looking for, there were more feathers than any bird can afford to lose, and a child's voice-changer toy that didn't seem to work.

They never got to the bottom of the Kris > Crystal > Hendrix triangle, but somebody somewhere will be texting left-handed for the rest of their life.

Ivan

Ivan was born angry. He emerged from his egg with a bee in his bonnet, a chip on his shoulder and all of the other appropriate idioms that might describe him as a Bit Of A Dick. He fought his way through the other chicks for his food, he built 'walls'[198] around his nighttime spot and fiercely defended them against invaders. He strutted so that he appeared bigger than the other chicks and was not afraid to put holes in them if they invaded his personal space. He was not a nice chick.

He got bigger, and his voracious appetite and bullying behaviour meant that he quickly overtook the others in size and became the big fish in a small pond. He was 'spotted' by the farmer in charge of the incubator, and removed from the comfort of his sawdust fort. He put up a fight though, making several perforations in the hand of the woman holding him but she didn't let go.

Held securely in her largely clenched fist, Ivan was whisked away to a building with 'breeding programme' written on the door. His new home was in a small enclosure with a heat lamp and some food, along with six other young male chickens who were just as territorial as he was, which made feeding time messy. Ivan was a bit bigger than them and on day two he had his first fight, fought over feed. He won, and the other bird lost enough of his anatomy to make him even

---

[198] They were made of sawdust. Even the Three Little Pigs didn't build walls out of sawdust, but he was making the most of what he had; shit and sawdust. I realise the phrase is normally 'spit and sawdust' but shit was what Ivan had.

more flightless than an average chicken, at the hands[199] of Ivan's feet.

Ivan was Big Fish again and he loved it. Day three saw a total bloodbath; Ivan wasn't prepared to share his food and he attacked the first bird who made a pass at it. Through luck more than judgement, he caught the artery running down the other chicken's neck with one claw, and it bled to death on the floor. The others then joined forces and surrounded him, apparently keen to avenge their partner. They were all still very young, and none of them would, after this encounter with Ivan, get any older.

What happened next was like a scene out of an 18+ spoof horror movie, because the demise of the other teenage boy chickens was so gory and so unlikely that it couldn't possibly have happened… but it did[200]. One of them ended up choking on the lower leg of another, which was no longer attached. A second (the one which had already lost a wing) had its own eyeballs inserted in its cloaca. A third had been disemboweled, its entrails spread around the enclosure like lumpy jam. A fourth bled to death from the stumps of its wings, as it jumped around like both of its feet were pogo sticks and sprayed blood a much greater distance than should have been possible. The final casualty had tried to escape by climbing up the bars of the enclosure. Ivan had grabbed it by the feet and pulled, whilst it was trying to climb through the bars. It had broken its neck and lost a foot at the same time.

---

[199] Metaphorical hands, obviously.

[200] …except it didn't, because this is a work of fiction. Not even lifelike fiction.

When the farmer came to feed the juveniles the following day, she was greeted by a single, smug looking bird which was not going to be picked up. Where she would normally have gone in to fill the feed dispenser, this time she threw some handfuls of feed in from a safe distance, and thought about what the future might hold for this beast.

Ivan had originally been separated from the other chicks because he was big and strong, which the farmer had thought would be a good trait for a breeding bird; 'big' normally equates with 'family sized roast'. In this instance, 'big' meant 'brutal' and there was no way that it was a good idea to unleash Ivan on the beautiful females of his flock, because the flock would cease to be a flock almost immediately. Ivan needed a new path.

The farmer[201] slept on it and dreamed of chickens and blood[202]. She woke up with a plan which required a tranquilliser dart and a small barn that nobody knows about.

He was subsequently isolated in his enclosure and fed on luxury scraps for several months until he reached his maximum size. He was magnificent, beautifully booted[203], a prominent and erect comb and spectacular plumage. He was a specimen of poultry masculinity, giant in size and in nature. Extra protein in his diet had served him well and his horrendous attitude had been amplified by isolation.

---

[201] She needs a name. We'll call her Clarissa.

[202] She would later fail a psychopath test, but that's a different story.

[203] This is genuinely the term for having feathers around legs. If only pretty coloured feathers were called 'suited' then you could say a cockerel was 'suited and booted'.

Clarissa built a large log cabin in a corner of her farm, behind a dense hedge, in an area which had been where farm machinery went to die. There were no windows, and CCTV looked out in all directions from the roof. In the centre of the cabin was a small enclosure, 2m square with a low fence around the edge and sawdust on the floor. This would become the cockpit of Clarissa's new enterprise.

She spread the word very quietly, using her uncomfortably knowledgable son to access the Dark Web and her father to discuss quietly in dark bars in and around the area. A date was set, and there was a quiet buzz in anticipation of something exciting on the horizon.

The day came. Seven pickup trucks with cages in the back arrived and countless other people came by car, bike and scooter. The cabin filled up and lots of money changed hands. Two birds were put in the cockpit, rubbed together, and then released. There was screaming and shouting for eight minutes, then one of the birds lost its battle and lay down, bleeding heavily.

More money changed hands.

Two birds were retired[204] and two more entered the cockpit. They shouted at each other, circled a lot and then fought to the death. This one was different because the fatal blow came to both birds at the same time, so they keeled over simultaneously in a pool of collective blood. This was a massive win for the bookies because it meant that **everyone**[205] lost.

---

[204] One permanently - it became three dinners and a lunch.

[205] Except the bookies of course - they never lose.

The process repeated while Ivan got more and more irritable in his tiny box. This was, of course, exactly the point.

His debut fight was meant to be the highlight of the evening because he was an absolute monster. The odds were very much in his favour, and he did not disappoint. He ripped his opponent (literally) to pieces within two minutes, which was something of a record. There wasn't a mark on him and he strutted around his dead quarry with pride, oozing 'I am awesome' vibes.

At the end of the evening, he was shooed back into his cage and taken back to the barn. He slept. He would have licked his wounds if he had any, but he didn't[206].

For the next week, Ivan paced in his enclosure for hour after hour, his levels of irritability climbing with every passing step. He started to grumble and take his frustrations out on his enclosure; he pecked and kicked and generally hurled himself at the sides. Chicken housing is generally not designed to enclose angry champion fighting cocks, and Ivan quickly discovered where and how hard to kick.

He found his way back into the breeding room. Amongst the ladies, you might expect that his masculine urges[207] would be different but you would be disappointed. He chased the first chicken he saw and ripped her apart, then took it upon himself to wipe out the entire flock, one jugular at a time.

---

[206] Plus the difficulty raised by a chicken's incapacity to lick - short tongues.

[207] If they were people, this would be an excellent opportunity to demonstrate that not all men are violent and not all men are oversexed. Chickens do not adhere to feminist ideals.

They scattered and ran around like headless chickens[208] whilst he took them on one at a time. Clarissa heard the clamour for survival, dropped her tractor keys and ran to the barn, where she found another massacre. She cornered Ivan and threw a net over his head, which tangled him up enough that she could gather his feet and secure his beak for long enough to get him back into the cockpit, which was much more sturdy.

This became his home and he won every fight that came his way, with bells on. The odds were high, so people kept coming, ever hopeful that their cock was bigger and better than him. They were always wrong.

He got stronger, and more brutal. He tied knots in the intestines of his foes and did keepy-uppies with assorted body parts. He attacked owners, spectators and anything that looked like it might move. He developed an exceptional reputation among the cock-fighting community and was something of a celebrity, although strangely nobody wanted a selfie with him.

The tiny segment of Ivan's brain which was human meant that Ivan had enough cunning and guile to beat birds even bigger than him. His winning streak seemed endless…

…until it didn't.

It was a Saturday night and the bets had rolled in. There was a queue of angry roosters waiting to be unleashed on their nemesis and Ivan was ready for them. He pawed at the ground with his massive talons and puffed himself up to his considerable height.

---

[208] For some, the resemblance was uncanny…

Moments before the first bout was set to begin, a tiny ball of fluff found its way into the pit. It was one of the freshly hatched chicks, just a few days old, clumsy and stupid[209]. It was so small that it hopped under the fence without even bowing its head. It cheeped and flapped and fell over, and the room fell silent.

It was one thing to watch grown adult cockerels who were bred for no other purpose than to rip each other to pieces, but it was different when there was a baby involved. Especially when the baby was so incredibly cute. Nobody moved. Every soul in the room wanted to rescue the plucky fluffball but not one of them was brave enough to step into the ring.

Ivan took three steps towards the tiny chick. It wobbled a bit closer to Ivan. Ivan leaned forward in what most chickens would recognise as a menacing way. The chick's fluff ruffled as Ivan breathed on her. Every human in the room held their breath and prayed to whatever god they could think of.

The chick looked up into two massive eyes that were blazing with an unquenched thirst for blood; if it were a cartoon then there would have been flames coming out of Ivan's eye sockets.

"Peep?"

Whatever flames were burning in Ivan were extinguished by that ridiculous noise. He leaned further forward and picked the chick up in his beak. The assembled company took a collective gasp, expecting him to throw the chick in the air or swallow her in one gulp, or something else similarly

---

[209] This describes all chickens, to be fair.

brutal. Perhaps he might tear her wings off or turn her inside out.

None of these things happened. In fact, Ivan took her to a corner of the cockpit[210] and put his wing around her. There was a long, confused pause while the spectators processed what was happening in front of them. There was a chicken in the ring with Ivan, which made this a prospective fight. It was also Ivan's first ever loss and there were a lot of very large bets to be settled. Whilst everyone was thoroughly discombobulated, they were also counting their betting slips because a loss meant a lot of big payouts for those that had placed a one in a million bet on Ivan losing.

For a short period of time, there was a clamour for cash and nobody was particularly interested in Ivan, who was tucked into a corner[211], still and silent.

…then he took his wing from around the chick, and everyone froze. Nobody made a sound; several people for close to passing out because they hadn't yet remembered to breathe.

In one swift, fluid movement, Ivan grabbed the chick and threw her high in the air.

---

[210] I've let this slip so far but a cockfighting ring really **is** called a cockpit. It's probably best that this is not confused with the cockpit of an aeroplane; that could be an actual disaster.

[211] This is yet another lie. Cockpits are circular and anyone who's ever attended a maths lesson knows that circles don't have corners.

Time stood still[212].

The chick somersaulted through the air at about eight frames per second, its glassy eyes catching those of the assembled crowd, one at a time.

Still, nobody moved[213].

The negligent movement carried on for a bit longer.

The chick reached the apex of its voyage and began its descent.

43 eyes[214] watched as she spun slowly in the air.

She landed smartly on Ivan's back, in a spot that was apparently made for her tiny frame; it almost looked like a saddle. At this point, Ivan connected with his Inner Horse and galloped headlong towards the other end of the arena. One bound of his giant legs (and a small amount of surprisingly elegant flapping) and he cleared the fence.

The people on the other side of the fence parted, and Ivan was like Moses in the Red Sea[215] and he galloped towards the fortuitously open door. He kept galloping, and his rider

---

[212] It didn't really - that's impossible, which means it can't happen in a story about a human chicken. Couldn't have something impossible in such a credible story, could we?!

[213] Although those who had previously held their breath rethought their life choices, in an attempt to make it out alive.

[214] One of the spectators had been in an unfortunate accident with a mountaineering hamster. What a brilliant story for the staff in Eye A&E.

[215] I'll let you decide which of these two stories is more credible…

held on for dear life with her beak and her sharp little feet. They sped through the farmyard and out onto the main road, like characters in an ill thought out cartoon.

When Ivan's lungs began to rebel against overuse, he figured it might be prudent to stop, so they stopped. His charge[216] dismounted - or fell off - and they sat in a gap in the hedge. Ivan found some worms and gently presented them to Bee, who had never been in a situation where her food moved before. She squeaked and jumped backwards, convinced that this 2cm pink thing was a ferocious enemy. Ivan put his sizeable foot on the worm, carved it in two, and offered one half to Bee. She pecked at it, and that was another problem solved.

Ivan had been angry for his whole short life, but had never had anything to be particularly happy about. He had a purpose now. A little someone who needed him. Without him, Bee didn't have the slightest chance in this world that she didn't understand.

And so Angry Ivan became Overprotective Dad Ivan. He showed Bee how to survive, kept her warm, and in return she gave him purpose. His reputation meant that stories of The Beast appeared in the news from time to time, and - if he could read - he would have laughed hysterically at the astonishing inaccuracy of modern reporting.

If the newspapers were to be believed, he had murdered entire families, burned down a children's hospital and stolen a fleet of cars. He was single-handedly[217] wiping out the

---

[216] Oooooh. How about Bee as an illogical name for a chick?

[217] Yes, it hasn't escaped my notice that chickens don't have hands, but 'single-footedly' isn't a phrase.

population of the entire county. Perhaps the country; rumours are impressive.

Anyway. They lived out their life in surprising anonymity, through Spring, Summer and the beginning of Winter. It snowed, and although Bee was almost fully grown, she still didn't cope well with the cold. In his capacity as her guardian, Ivan felt he should find a way to warm her up and keep her safe.

They found a house. There was an intense beeping noise; the owners of the house had an inappropriately installed heat detector[218] and had just cooked a set of jacket potatoes. To clear the alarm they had opened the door to encourage some air flow. This was great news for Ivan and Bee.

As the family retired to the living room to eat their spuds and watch a long but spellbinding film, Ivan and Bee found a warm spot in the kitchen to rest in.

The oven was still on. A small crust of potato skin was festering on the bottom of the oven, along with several months of congealed ming[219]. The oven was on its highest setting, which was too high. The ming was a combination of water, fat and unrecognisable food scraps that had been there since the dawn of time. All of the best bits of Chemistry and Physics combined in perfect harmony…

---

[218] Some fool had installed it directly above the oven, so every time someone cooked something, the neighbours thought there was a fire. There was almost **never** a fire.

[219] If minging can be an adjective, then surely it can also be a noun? Could it also be a verb? Can a person ming as well as **be** minging?

...and then there were flames.

The alarm was such a normal feature of the household that anyone within hearing distance had frankly stopped hearing it, so no eyelids were batted when it started blaring again.

To Ivan and Bee, flames were warm and flames were pretty. These were two attributes that they appreciated but totally misunderstood. The inside of the oven was well and truly on fire, and the hinges of the oven door failed[220]. Splashes of hot oil escaped onto the tea towel that was hanging on the over door. It caught fire. It fell to the floor, and the vinyl floor tiles also caught fire, which spread to the rest of the kitchen.

Bee squeaked with joy because she had been frozen stiff just a few minutes before and now she was lovely and warm. Ivan had slightly more brainpower than Bee and recognised that none of this was good news. Using a spatula and a can of beans, and without warning, Bee was catapulted through the open door into the frost outside, and the rest of her life.

Ivan, on the other hand, became roast chicken.

---

[220] This is really bad science, and would not happen in real life, but I still I recommend that you clean your oven before it is colonised by other lifeforms.

Norah

The overhead heater was hot, and Norah erupted into the world feeling like a reassembled set of chicken drumsticks[221]. She rolled around about until she was away from the blazing inferno above her and lay on her back looking convincingly dead. Another (less dead) chick ran over what it thought was her corpse, and snapped her out of the brief coma she had fallen into.

5 weeks and counting

She stood up. She ate. She grew. She kept away from the insanity that was the rest of the brood, and grew some more. After two days, they were all moved to a shed, sectioned off into different areas, each one populated by chickens of different sizes. They were crammed in like sardines with feathers and Norah was no longer able to have any semblance of personal space. The second her feet hit the ground there were others bouncing over her head, trampling her, knocking her over, pecking at her and generally reminding her that chickens are not solitary creatures.

It was dark in the shed. While there were small windows, they generally had something roosting in them, which blocked out what little light there was. There was a row of feeders through the middle of the barn, which magically spewed out seed every few hours. Norah ate whatever was left over when the other 4,000 chicks had finished, and drank from the water drippers. She tried to perch when she could and flapped her wings whenever there was enough space to stretch them out.

---

[221] Very small ones; not much of a meal.

It was not an exciting, inspiring or fulfilling life. It was brutal and painful and incredibly dull.

4 weeks and counting

Nothing changed, really.

One of the adjoining subdivisions of the shed was cleared out; Norah watched the chickens being picked up one at a time by the feet and put into crates. The floor was swept, cleaned out with a pressure washer, and then a fresh batch of fluffy chicks was dumped in to replace the older ones that had left. Norah had a sense that it was a permanent departure and a short term tenancy.

She had grown quite fast and had a competitive advantage over most of the others, which meant there was a perch that mostly had her name on it, giving her a little breathing[222] space. She watched when the farmer occasionally came in for a 'welfare check', and she made sure she was high enough to see what happened every time one of the sheds was opened.

There were often casualties; birds which had been trampled, pecked or had got sick. Sometimes some just seemed to give up on life and lie down in protest at the whole concept of life. Those that didn't make it were swept up by the farmer during a 'welfare check' and taken away in a big sack. She watched carefully. She learned a lot.

3 weeks and counting

---

[222] And flapping

Another few batches of birds were caught and carried away. Norah couldn't help but feel like she was losing thousands of brothers and sisters every day and she was running out of heartstrings to be tugged at.

There was no way out of the barn; the windows were solid and the fences between sections of the shed were made of chicken wire[223] whose holes were smaller than chickens. Without significant self-mutilation, the fence was not an option. The door opened once a day at a specific time, and there was a small lobby area before the doors to each part of the barn. Any chicken that had the misfortune to ooze out into the lobby found its way back in, courtesy of a pair of steel toe-caps.

2 weeks and counting

Norah had worked out that The Gathering happened at 5 weeks, and figured out that she had two weeks left before she found out whether she was right about the fate of her siblings. This wasn't a hypothesis that she was enthusiastic about testing and she only had 14 days to find an alternative life plan. She found that meditation[224] helped her to drown out the stench and the screaming and spent every waking minute[225] trying to find a way out or a way through.

1 week and counting

For Norah, time was literally running out. She felt like a convict waiting for its last rites, whose last meal was

---

[223] The clue is in the name

[224] Sitting very still on a perch and hoping that everything will go away.

[225] …and some sleeping ones…

destined to be exactly the same as every other. If she had tallied every lost bird on the wall like they do in the movies, there would have been no wall left and she would have moved on to the ceiling and floor already. Instead of counting, she thought until her tiny brain hurt.

The gathering

On the day of The Gathering, Norah's time was already up. The farmer found her lifeless on the floor, shouted "I've found dinner" to someone outside, and stuffed Norah into a bag. That was it for Norah.

Except it wasn't, because Norah was an excellent actor in the circumstances. She had held her breath for long enough that she passed out, and the others trampled on her to the point where she was almost dead for real, but her thready pulse endured. She was poured out of the bag onto a kitchen counter in a utility room. Big hands took hold of her and the torture began; every feather was painstakingly[226] ripped out and her increasingly cold body[227] was left to 'rest'.

Life

Norah woke up cold, naked and confused, but free. 'Cold' was the most pressing of those things; her entire insulation system was in a pile next to her, and the only apparent form

---

[226] The pain was entirely for Norah. Fortunately she was unconscious and missed the worst part of her ordeal.

[227] This is presumably where the term 'goosebumps' comes from. A cursory glance at the internet would probably tell me for sure but I don't care enough to look. Perhaps this is the beginning of a new urban myth.

of warming on offer was a casserole dish with pretty little flowers and a large dose of rosemary.

She hopped down from the counter and felt the urge to cover what would have been her crotch if she were a person. I cannot stress enough how ridiculous a naked chicken looks, running around a kitchen floor[228] and Norah was somehow managing to body-shame herself. There was a tea towel hanging on a hook, and she managed to wrap it around herself like a teenager going to a toga party, but without the vomit.

Another stroke of luck was the cat flap in the back door, which she hopped through with relative ease. Less lucky was Horatio the cat, who was sunning himself on the other side. When the naked chicken appeared, Horatio immediately made himself big like only a very small cat can, puffing up his fur and arching his back. He thought briefly about attacking Norah, but losing her feathers made her beak and claws look so much longer and so much pointier[229]. Her nakedness also made him uneasy; this was a scenario that did not feature in kitten training.

He turned and walked away, with the air of a cat who wants the world to think he **chose** to walk away and is in no way scared, whilst trying to hide the fact that he was quivering in his fur. He made what he thought was a brave and nonchalant retreat, occasionally looking back to check that he wasn't being followed. Norah trotted after him as though he'd just thrown a stick for her and when he gave up on the

---

[228] Or anywhere else. It's not kitchen floor specific.

[229] Apparently, this is why people often shave their pubic hair. They probably look marginally less ridiculous than a naked chicken wearing a tea-towel toga.

last traces of his pride and broke into a gentle jog she started running too. When he opened out his stride into an actual plea for freedom, she did the same but on fewer legs. This was not a race that Norah was going to win, especially when Horatio remembered he could climb, and Norah realised that she really couldn't.

She adjusted her toga and headed out onto the open road. She saw a bus, and climbed on - she even had the audacity to wave at Horatio, who waved back[230]. With no idea where the bus was going, and nothing but a toga to hide her modesty, the next adventure began.

She hid under a seat next to a small child who had just been shopping with his grandparents, and had bought a teddy bear and several outfits for it. He caught a glimpse of Norah's toga and pulled on it, at which point she popped out from under the chair as he unravelled her. She was shivering and hungry, and he was a very well brought up child. Without a second thought, he silently offered her one of the teddy outfits in his bag, and she nodded in grateful acceptance. It's very difficult to dress yourself when you have no hands, so the lad held the shorts for her to step into, and opened up an oversized jumper so she could slide her stumpy little wings in. He strapped something around her neck, and tapped her bumpy head with his little hand. She nodded, rubbed against his leg, and tucked back under the seat.

At the next stop, Norah hopped off the bus and found herself on a busy shopping street. She caused a stir right from the beginning, people forming a circle around her and stopping to watch. Some of them got their phones out to

---

[230] In so doing, he forgot to hold on and fell out of the tree.

film her or take photos. One bearded beauty even braved a selfie, lying down on the ground next to her so that he could be in the shot.

Norah knew that a naked chicken was a novelty but she wasn't aware of the full story; she didn't know that they knew more than she did. Enjoying the limelight, she did a pirouette, and a little dance. The crowd loved it; there were laughs and shouts and a raucous round of applause. Someone put some music through the tinny speaker of their phone and she got into her groove, which only made the crowd bigger. A child in a pushchair was eating popcorn, and she did something a big like a cartwheel in his general direction, ending up on his lap and tucking in. He was delighted and more than happy to share, while she gorged herself on Sweet and Salty.

When she'd had enough, she dropped to the floor and took a bow - another popular choice. The crowd roared. Norah strutted off down the street; the crowd parted to let her past, and then followed her; she was like the Pied Piper in chicken form, charming the locals in whatever town the bus had dropped her off in. Totally oblivious to what the fuss was **really** about, she ducked under a hedge[231] and found a bush to hide in for the night. All was good with the world.

The sun came up and Norah began her second day of celebrity. Unbeknownst to her, she had a reputation already. News bulletins were raving about her, children were talking about her in school and photographers were poised on every street corner, hoping to catch a shot of the not-so-naked-bird.

---

[231] It was a hawthorn hedge. People stopped following her.

The sun was warm, there was a gentle breeze and half a sandwich lay unmolested under a picnic table. The discovery that it was a chicken sandwich nearly broke Norah, who hadn't foreseen cannibalism in her future and abandoned the sandwich. It wasn't long before someone saw her and bought her some luxury[232] birdseed, and used it to tempt her into their car.

She perched on the dashboard, watching the world whiz by. Pedestrians were delighted when they saw her drive by and she was certain that her magnetic personality and outstanding movement skills were the reason for her fame. She was wrong.

The driver of the car jammed the brakes on when a child stepped into the road, and Norah slammed into the windscreen. All the air was knocked out of her body and she made a noise a bit like a squeaky dog toy. She flopped back onto the seat and the driver pulled over.

He reached over to a little box on the dashboard, and pressed a button. He looked at his phone, scrolled a bit and did a fist-pump.

"Got it!"

Norah didn't know what exactly it was that he'd got, but hopped onto his lap and found him on social media, just as he hit 'upload'. She didn't see what he'd uploaded but would later discover that it was slow motion dash cam

---

[232] Mealworms made it 'luxury' apparently.

footage of Norah's interaction with the windscreen[233]. She went viral and still had no idea what the fuss was all about.

She was taken to a house, where the driver of the car put her in his spare bedroom with a tray of random food and put the radio on. She ate a grape, half a packet of crisps, something brown, and a jelly sweet. The jelly sweet was a mistake, sticking in her throat until she turned a funny colour[234]. A vague recollection of first aid principles made her throw herself at a wall in an attempt to dislodge the sweet, which she managed on the third attempt. In true slapstick style, the sweet gained its liberty at exactly the same moment as the house owner opened the door, hitting (and sticking to) his forehead in the most unlikely fashion. He left again. There was too much about this day that made his head hurt and a rogue half chewed sweet was a step too far.

Norah had never slept in a bed before[235] but the sheets were soft and warm and the pillow was like she thought a marshmallow would be like if you slept on it. The radio rambled on quietly in the background and Norah dreamed of crisps.

She woke up to the 'DaDeDaDaaaaargh' jingle that preceded the morning news.

---

[233] This is a significant continuity error because dash cams face forwards; what use could they possibly be if they were aimed **inside** the car? But let's not let accuracy get in the way of a good story.

[234] People genuinely turn blue-grey when they're starved of oxygen. I have no idea what colour chickens turn, and I don't care enough to look it up. We'll just go with blue.

[235] Because she was a chicken. Just in case you forgot.

"Superchicken has taken the world by storm, after his viral car stunt yesterday. People are flocking into town to try and get a glimpse of his next trick, but his whereabouts are as yet unknown. In other news, tomatoes and cucumbers are out of stock again everywhere[236], although there are rumours of orange peppers in the mini-mart on the high street. Fajitas may yet be back on the menu!"

They couldn't be referring to Norah - Norah was a 'she' not a 'he'. Or could they? Do people know the difference between a 'he chicken' and a 'she chicken'? Was she wearing a blue outfit with something like 'top man' on the back? She hadn't given her outfit a second thought; perhaps that was the reason she was being misgendered and the news reader really was referring to her as the internet sensation.

There was a mirror on the wall; she could see the reflection of the light fitting in it from the bed but wasn't tall enough to be able to look into it. She tried bouncing on the bed and although it was the most fun she'd ever had, it didn't help her to see more than the top of her head.

The bedroom door was open and she ventured out into the house, determined to find a mirror in which she could see what a naked chicken looked like. She flap-jumped onto the side of the bath and from there to the edge of the sink, which proved to be less easy to hold on to than she thought. For her second effort, she landed **in** the sink instead, tantalisingly close to the mirror above the sink but still not able to see into it. She couldn't jump because her feet scrabbled around in the sink like a puppy trying to run on a wet tiled floor.

---

[236] If you know, you know.

It was time to accept defeat on this mirror and move on to a third. Further exploration took her out onto the landing, where a full length mirror at the top of the stairs took her by surprise. The vision that greeted her was absolutely, categorically and definitely 'superchicken'. The outfit that kind little boy had kitted her out with was a superhero outfit with a huge yellow 'S' on the chest. The thing that he had strapped around her neck was a cape.

Now she understood why people had been so transfixed by her. Who **wouldn't** want to see a naked chicken dressed as a superhero and dancing to nondescript pop music? She 100% deserved her 'headline' status.

What next? She was famous. She was an actual celebrity. Not only that, but she was the first celebrity chicken in history which surely made her even more special. Was she on the TV news and in the newspapers? Was she a global sensation?

She'd been taken up the stairs under the arm of the person whose house she was in, so going down them solo was a new experience and not her finest hour. She landed at the bottom somewhat unceremoniously then embarked on a tour of the rest of the house. She found a sofa, installed herself on it, and pressed every button on the remote control until something appeared on the TV screen.

Some time later, Sigibert[237] came home to find Norah on his sofa like she'd lived there her whole life, watching a cooking show (which mercifully didn't involve a chicken dish). He

---

[237] Sigi for short, because it's a tiny bit less daft. Apologies to every Sigibert in the world. Your parents must be terrible people.

took a photo, before kneeling down until he was at eye level with Norah.

"Hi! I'm Sigibert. Pleased to make your acquaintance[238]" - then he extended his hand, which she waggled her stumpy wing at in the closest thing to a handshake that she could manage. He was surprised by this response[239] and there was a brief pause in proceedings.

"Are you hungry?"

She nodded.

"Do you like bread?"

She shook her head. She didn't really know what 'bread' was but she didn't think she wanted it.

"...er... How about scrambled eggs? Wait... no... you're a chicken... Cereal?"

Cereal sounded better somehow and Sigi dutifully fetched some small colourful hoops in a bowl. Norah plunged in and was foiled by the hoop that wrapped itself around her beak. She could smell the food and see the food, but she couldn't **eat** the food. She looked up at Sigi with sadness in her eyes and - in between bouts of hysterical laughter - he released Norah from her wheaty prison. He reached into the bowl

---

[238] The only people who talk like this are Americans, pretending to be English, in badly written films. My apologies.

[239] If he wasn't expecting a response, why did he put his hand out? Stupid man...

and crushed the remaining hoops with one giant[240] hand so that she could enjoy the rest of her breakfast. She did.

He watched her eat, clumsily chasing the last few dry pieces around the bowl until every crumb was gone. He took the bowl back into the kitchen, rinsed it, and put a small amount of water in the bottom. Norah took a glug, feeling as though the cereal had sucked every last drop of moisture out of her; the water was gratefully received.

Norah's clothes were looking tired; they were designed for teddy bears who generally don't go walking, don't toss around in their sleep or eat breakfast. The shorts had split down the back and their colour suggested that they were full of second hand food. There were crumbs everywhere and the cape was just tatty. He started to undress her but she flapped and pecked him in protest. He tried again, and she pecked harder.

"But your clothes are falling apart and filthy!" She covered her eyes with wings that were only just long enough to reach her face, then did something that looked a bit like a shrug,

"Oh I see! You're embarrassed! I'm so sorry!" He turned away and took off all three items of clothing without looking. In the process he poked her in the eye, knocked her off the sofa and got chicken shit all over both himself and his beige sofa. She parked herself back on the sofa, and smeared it around some more, but he was blissfully unaware because he was still looking the other way. The clothes went into the washing machine and Sigi went back to the living room with a tea towel to cover her modesty, then he scooped her up

---

[240] It wasn't really a giant hand but Norah was a small chicken.

and took her to the bathroom for some much needed ablutions.

He put a few centimetres of warm water into the bath and some bubbles and left the room.

For obvious reasons, Norah had never had a bath before and had no idea why she'd been locked in the bathroom[241] or what she was meant to do next. She hopped onto the side of the bath, lost her grip and fell into the bath. The ensuing chaos spread a fabulous combination of excrement and lavender-scented bubbles around the room. If she had still been blessed with feathers, the carnage would have been infinitely worse. The sides of the bath were slippery and panic levels rose with every attempt to get out until eventually she collapsed into the warm water, exhausted but fragrant.

As she tried to get her breath back, she started to appreciate the warmth of the water and the calming scent of the lavender. She lay back and realised that she was floating, a totally new sensation. She waggled her wing stumps slightly and found that she moved around when she did. She waggled faster, and moved faster. She waggled one more than the other and changed direction. She waggled one wing harder and it flipped her over so she was face down in the water, whereupon she quickly discovered that chickens do not have gills.

More frantic flapping righted her and drenched a bit more of the bathroom. Lesson learned. Oblivious to the shards of

---

[241] The door wasn't actually locked but without hands, a circular doorknob more than 30cm off the ground may as well be a locked door.

shit floating around her head, Norah enjoyed her bath and her bubbles.

Sigi returned after about half an hour to an entirely redecorated bathroom. The 'theme' was 'bubble' with a hint of 'bowel contents'. No interior designer in the history of interior design would have walked into that room with "Wow, I like what you've done with the place". Sigi added to the decor by throwing up, and did it in style. He lurched towards the sink, slipped on the extensive bubbly floor-hazard and the vomit fountain begun mid flight. His semi-digested breakfast spread up the wall, spattered on the window and there was a smattering of cornflakes in the bath water.

Norah ate them.

Sigi scraped the bits out of his hair and rinsed his face in the sink. He changed his clothes and put the soiled ones straight into the washing machine. He had no words, so he pulled the plug out of the bath and turned the over-bath shower on to get the chunks[242] off Norah, once again turning away. She enjoyed the 'rain' and when she was clean(er) he wrapped her in a fluffy towel to save her blushes[243] and took her back downstairs. Remembering the stains she'd left on the sofa, he installed her on an armchair, wrapped up in her towel - ironically[244] trussed up like a chicken.

After taking a necessary shower himself, he applied his thoughts to Norah's wardrobe problems. Strangely, he didn't

---

[242] (food in various stages of digestion)

[243] She had no **actual** blushes - these were metaphorical ones.

[244] Someone somewhere will undoubtedly complain that this isn't accurate use of the word 'ironically'. I could not give a shit.

have any chicken clothes in his wardrobe; **nobody** has chicken clothes in their wardrobe because 'chicken clothes' are not a 'thing'. He had no children or children's clothes, and no sewing expertise that might fill the gap. He found an old oversized jumper, and snipped two holes on either side of the cuffs for Norah's wings and two smaller holes further down for her legs. He left it long enough that the rest of the jumper would cover her tail. It would have to do.

Norah wriggled into what would become a badly fitted dress, and our two newly hygienic friends were ready for a trip. Sigi decided that his biggest priority was clothes, and headed straight for the teddy-bear shop as a short term solution. He explained the situation to Norah, who seemed happy and then gave her free rein to choose her outfits, hoping that his credit card would hold up to the strain. She chose:

- A sparkly pink dress because it was sparkly; what's not to like?
- A cowboy outfit with a fine black hat, because the hat was awesome.
- An all-in-one rabbit suit, mainly for the comedy value[245].
- A Hawaiian shirt and shorts which didn't match at all because she liked the colours but had zero fashion sense.
- A satin dressing gown that made her look like a boxer[246], because she thought it made her look kick-ass.

---

[245] A person, who thinks it's a chicken, pretending to be a rabbit. Familiar territory.

[246] I feel I should qualify this. She looked **nothing** like a real boxer; she just looked like a naked chicken-boxer would look if chicken-boxing was an Olympic sport.

- A superhero costume based on a movie which I probably shouldn't mention for legal reasons…[247]
- A wizard's robe which had a wonderful beard attached to it, because who **doesn't** want to look like a wizard??
- A suit and bow tie, for special occasions.
- A wedding dress; just in case she met Mr Perfect.
- An anorak because she didn't think she'd like rain.

Sigi looked away when the bill appeared on the screen of the card machine because he knew it would cause him physical pain if he saw it. He would have been right.

Norah was too small to run along beside Sigi, so he perched her on his shoulder and tried to ignore the very real possibility that a trail of chicken shit was working its way down his back. They went straight to the toilets in the shopping centre they were in, and guiltily headed for the 'family' room, where Sigi helped Norah into the cowboy outfit. The hat was a bit big and was ultimately dangling down her back, but she was undoubtedly the coolest chicken in town.

Everywhere they went thereafter, they drew gasps, laughter, cheers and copious pointing events from adults and children alike. Norah held on tightly to Sigi's shoulder[248] and they were treated to VIP treatment when they went for a burger together. Out of respect, Sigi opted not to have the chicken burger. Norah had half of a corn on the cob with butter. She discovered she loved chips.

---

[247] …but it was shiny and it had pointy ears.

[248] Tiny holes at the front and back of one shoulder were testament to exactly how tightly Norah was holding on.

That evening, sitting on the clean half of the sofa together, Norah and Sigi realised they were on the news. There were clips of them walking through town, and a very cute clip of Sigi wiping butter off most of Norah. It was exciting; neither of them had experienced celebrity status before. They did a little[249] high-five and - when the news finished - Sigi took Norah up the stairs and tucked her into bed.

A new day dawned and Norah could hear Sigi on the phone downstairs. By the time she had thrown herself down the stairs, he had already booked them onto an evening chat show. Norah didn't really know what a 'chat show' was but Sigi was happy so she tried to look excited. He spent the rest of the morning chatting to her about life, the universe, and the price of wheat. Norah was largely a bystander in these discussions; had she been a person, her facial expression would have enabled her to join in, but chickens don't really 'do' facial expressions…[250] She nodded a lot and shrugged occasionally. At one point, she laid a conciliatory wingtip on his arm, although she wasn't entirely sure what she was consoling him about because she couldn't entirely follow the conversation. It was a bit like having a conversation with someone in French, when you've only got a couple of years of secondary school French under your belt, and the other person in the conversation is babbling at several billions words per second.

For the next few days, stuff happened. Not interesting stuff - just run-of-the-mill life stuff, mainly involving domesticity

---

[249] **Very** little - her wings were only about 7cm long without feathers.

[250] For good reason. Facial expressions require eyebrows, lips and - occasionally - nostrils. These are not anatomically appropriate in the chicken world.

and sleep, punctuated by food and housetraining. Ordinary life to Sigi, extraordinary life to Norah.

The evening of the chat show came around. They went to London by train - the channel even paid for a first class seat. The irony was that they were guaranteed a seat, and Norah's diminutive backside took up about 7% of it. Apart from that they had a bit more leg room (again - hardly relevant when your legs are less than the length of a chicken drumstick[251]. They also got a free coffee and a horrendous sandwich.

At the studio, Norah discovered the joys of wardrobe and make up. The wardrobe staff were bemused and woefully unprepared for Norah. They had furnished a performing dog with a bow tie and had custom-made a colourful nappy for a chimp with overactive bowels. They had never needed to accessorise for a chicken before.

Whilst one of the staff busied around looking for foundation that was the right shade for chicken follicles, another shot off to a back room where the sounds of scissors and a sewing machine filled the silence, with a few expletives and ripping fabric. An unfeasibly short time later, the same face reappeared clutching a tiny fitted suit on a tiny hanger. It was attached by a sequence of tiny poppers down the back, and it looked like it had come straight out of a high-end department store. The operator of the sewing machine had **skills**.

---

[251] I realise that this is a cruel analogy.

Norah skipped behind a screen and thought about getting changed, remembered she had no hands and sheepishly[252] traipsed back out to seek support from a wardrobe assistant, who averted her gaze like a pro as Norah slipped out of a cowboy suit and into an actual suit.

They put makeup on her, which she didn't entirely see the point of. There was a comical moment when a keen but clearly junior team member took out a lipstick, moved towards her and realised that it wouldn't quite make sense on a beak. It wasn't a beakstick, after all. Eyeshadow was also surplus to requirements but nobody looked as uncomfortable as the hair artist who was very unhappy that there was nowhere to thrust his comb.

When the time came, they were called out onto the set by the hosts, because they thought there was comedy value in Norah trotting out, suited and booted. Sigi sat on the sofa and Norah stood by his feet, acutely aware that any graceful attempt to mount the sofa would lead to humiliating failure. She waited patiently until eventually one of the hosts leaned down and lifted her onto the seat, and she was greeted by lots of "ooooh" and "aaaah" noises.

"So what's it like living with this lovely guy?" asked one of the hosts.

In her head, Norah told them how kind he'd been and how much of a mess she'd made. She told them that her brother and sister chickens were all dead and that it was really shitty living on a chicken farm. Sadly, the sounds that came out of her ~~mouth~~ beak were gurgles and clucks. Realising that she

---

[252] Chickenishly? No. That is the worst of the made-up words that I have made up so far.

had not done any of her ideas justice, she shrugged. They laughed. Not quite what she had in mind, but it was a start.

She used a wingtip to point at where she thought her stomach probably was, and nodded. She climbed onto Sigi's lap, and nuzzled into him in the most affectionate way that she could without impaling him on her beak, then she reached up for a high-five and the audience got the idea.

"Are you enjoying being on the TV?" This was said in that patronising high-pitched voice reserved for small children and idiots. She leaned in to Norah as she said it, with a gormless look that showed she was not expecting a coherent response. When Norah nodded, the lights came on in the presenter's eyes and Norah could almost see the cogs turning in there. This was not what she was expecting.

"...Er... So... Have you been making friends?" She pointed at Sigi and rubbed against him like a new puppy might. She thought for a second, jumped down from the sofa and toddled off back to the wardrobe and makeup room off set, and pecked at the feet of the person who had so skilfully thrown together her outfit. She then grabbed a trouser leg with her beak and dragged the young lad towards the set. There was a degree of protestation but when Norah started corralling the youngster towards the cameras, he didn't really have much of a choice. He found himself on the sofa next to Sigi, blinking in the lights and with no idea which camera was working and what he was meant to do. Norah wrapped her wings around one leg, signalling that this was her second favourite person in the world.

"Oh! You make friends quickly! Who's this?"
"Jay..." Clearly not a person who wanted to be in the limelight. There was a pause while the presenter waited for

him to say something else but the sound of nervousness was silence. A period of awkwardness was not great for the cameras, so she turned back to Norah.

"...so how do you know each other??" Norah could **hear** the second question mark. She proudly pointed at her shiny new clothes with her wingtips and made the floor of the studio her catwalk, with a twirl and some impressive strutting. If she had any tail feathers, she would have waggled them proactively.

"You? Made that??" Again, the second question mark was audible. Without the need of any actual words, her face and tone of voice said *'Oh my god. You're a **boy** and you're only about twelve, but you sew better than I could in a billion years. How is this fair, and why are you in such a shitty job when you can make stuff like that?'*

There was another awkward pause. Norah broke the silence with a croak, and pointed back at the sofa. Sigi reached out an arm, and Norah skipped up it like a ramp. The wardrobe assistant scuttled away, looking devastated, while his manager thought about what she could promote him to. He was destined for great things if she could arrange a personality transplant for him.

The rest of the interview was mostly with Sigi; Norah curled up and went to sleep next to him, quietly evacuating her bowels as she slept. The contents of her digestive system oozed out onto the sofa, which was a challenge for the next guest; it was a volunteer firefighter who had rescued triplets from a fire. She spotted the brown goop seconds after she had committed to sit down, and after the point at which it was too late to take evasive action. There was a squelch that nobody but her heard, as Norah and Sigi emerged back outside into the afternoon sun.

That sparked the beginning of a year of unbridled joy, in which these two unlikely besties did some incredible things together, and made enough money for both of them to retire on[253]. They appeared in TV adverts, became internet sensations, attracted a lot of sponsorship through assorted social media channels and very short videos about their exploits. These are the edited highlights of that year:

- A cameo in a movie about rabbits.
- A trip to the pyramids, which Norah spent in a jacuzzi because it was too hot outside[254].
- An afternoon in a lecture theatre, for an animal psychology class. The lecturer couldn't answer **any** of the students' questions and ushered the visitors out at the first opportunity.
- A diving trip to the Indian Ocean, in which Norah discovered that swimming without feathers is like dancing without feet.
- A meal in an award-winning restaurant, who brought out a plate of worms without batting an eyelid. They were garnished with fresh basil.
- A trip on a quad bike. Strangely, there were no helmets that would fit on Norah's head, so Sigi upended one and she simply climbed in and peeked out over the top.
- What was meant to be a pony-trek, but the pony took an instant dislike to chickens and it turned into a pony-sprint. It took a while for the pony to realise that it couldn't outrun Norah, because she was literally attached; Sigi had made

---

[253] For Norah, this was a very tiny sum.

[254] So technically, for her, **not** a trip to the pyramids.

her a little harness for situations like this and she was strapped to the reins.
- A flight with a peregrine falcon. This was an accident; the falcon thought Norah would be a wonderful snack, and was not expecting her to perforate its underbelly. The 'trip' quickly became a 'fall', followed by a reminder that swimming was not a sensible leisure choice as Norah plunged into a duckpond.
- An evening at a climbing wall. Norah discovered that if she ran at the wall at full speed and timed her first jump right, she could run up the wall all the way to the top, bouncing from hand-hold to hand-hold. Whilst this was an impressive feat, she then discovered that returning to the ground was much more difficult. She had had virtually no capacity to fly **with** feathers Without them her flight path was vertical.
- Then there was the rooftop sunset.

At the anniversary of their meeting, Sigi took Norah to an incredibly tall[255] building (she was sick in the lift) to watch the sun go down. He didn't have many people skills and Norah was the closest he had ever had to a partner. Whilst he didn't find her attractive, he had come to see her as a very close friend and had shared the best moments of his life with her. He wanted a beautiful moment that they would never forget, so he took her to see the summer sun go down from the rooftop terrace of a Caribbean hotel on a secluded private beach. They had eaten a wonderful meal, Sigi had talked at Norah and she had gesticulated at him with their own basic version of sign language. They had a small lexicon but were able to converse to an extent.

---

[255] It wasn't really very tall at all, but lets not forget that Norah was only about 24cm tall, if she stretched her neck out. Two stories was - to her - very tall. This building was only three stories high.

Under different circumstances[256], it might have been a romantic moment.

Sigi took Norah to the edge of the roof terrace as the last embers of the sun began their descent on the horizon. In silence, they absorbed the beauty before them. The blue of the ocean, white ripples in the sand, the small island in the distance and the occasional bird swooping majestically in front of them. They listened to the swooshing of the ocean and the distant sounds of an acoustic guitar floating up to them on the wind. A boat slowly made its way out to sea and waves broke on the beach below. The final phase of the sunset went through a rainbow of colours which no artist could have done justice to, and then the stars slowly appeared in the sky as it went from turquoise to midnight blue[257]. Sigi wondered whether he could identify any constellations and realised that he couldn't. There was a shooting star, but they both missed it because a distraught parent was trying to catch a rampant toddler on the beach.

All of these things (apart from the toddler) came together in a perfect moment.

There were palm trees[258] on the beach, and they swooshed in the breeze. There were no other sounds; the birds were

---

[256] I.e. with two actual people.

[257] Confusingly, it wasn't midnight.

[258] They probably weren't really palm trees, but that's what we call **all** trees that grow on beaches. They could have been apple trees, for all I know. Or melon trees. Do melons even grow on trees?

roosting, the child had been folded[259] into a car seat and everyone else had found happy hour in a bar along the bay, It was just Sigi, Norah and a gentle breeze. Norah wasn't sure if the swooshing trees were getting swooshier or whether she just had nothing else to listen to.

Before long, it became apparent that the trees were indeed becoming swooshier. The wind was getting windier. The gusts were getting gustier. Unfortunately, as Norah saw the pavement rushing towards her face, she realised that she had not got flyier.

---

[259] ...literally kicking and screaming. If you have ever tried to strap an angry child into a car seat, you will know it's like knitting with snakes.

Sean

Sean was born in March, in a wooden chicken coop that was built and painted to look like a quaint wooden house. It had window boxes on the front[260], and the number 12 on the door, with two little glass windows which were absolutely filthy. Inside, the owner of the chickens (described by most as 'eccentric' had made some mock furniture; there were beds and a kids' wooden kitchen that had been repurposed. Ironically, the chickens had nested inside the oven.

There were two other eggs in the oven, both of which hatched shortly after Sean. His first memory would be an up-close-and-personal view of his mother's rear end. She continued to sit on him for the next two days and he grew to love the warmth and generally fluffiness of being sat on. Once his mother decided it was time for them to stand on their own two feet, Sean took every opportunity to snuggle underneath as much of her as he could get away with, which was not normal chicken behaviour. As Sean was not a normal chicken, it was entirely appropriate behaviour.

It was a happy brood; they were tucked up at night and had the run of a big garden during the day. There was a resident cat which was awful at catting[261] who prowled around the garden looking for dandelions to savage, and the full range

---

[260] This was a mistake. Every possible hint of life that might have been in them was literally rooted out by the resident chickens - there was barely even any soil in them. It was a nice idea, but ultimately a disaster,.

[261] Totally incapable of catching anything, incompetent at tree climbing, and maternal towards anything non-human. Hated people.

of garden environments to explore. The 8 chickens scrabbled around under trees and bushes, and found tasty morsels everywhere they went. As Sean grew, it became clear (to him at least) that food was his 'thing'.

Sean was an eating machine. He found worms everywhere he went, and seemed to have a sixth sense for when scraps were on their way out of the kitchen window. He dutifully waited at what he knew was the right time; sometimes he even caught things in mid-air. On occasion, the things he caught were actual food.

He had the perfect claws for scraping bark from trees, and a beak that could end a snail's miserable existence with one clinical swoop. He had an above average understanding of appetite, but other than that he was fairly dumb.

There was a nasty little boy who lived next door - his name was Darren. Whenever he got the chance, he threw stones at the chickens or shouted at them to frighten them. In fact, he terrorised them in whatever way squeaked into the mind of a psychopathic 7 year old. He was old enough to understand how to be an absolute bastard, but young enough to get away with it because he was 'just a child'. The perfect storm for a trainee serial killer.

When Sean had followed a wasp[262] out into the road, Darren had tried to shoo him into the path of a passing van. The van swerved into a puddle, soaking Darren and totally missing Sean, who was oblivious to the whole debacle. On another occasion, Darren had caught Sean and thrown him from a first floor window to test the 'theory' that chickens can't fly. Sean landed in a tree, where he found a wealth of

---

[262] He wasn't sharp enough to identify the potential pitfalls of a waspy snack…

bugs without ever realising that he had - once again - escaped certain death.

When missiles[263] were fired in his general direction, Sean always seemed to bend down, reach up or side step at exactly the right point to avoid ever being hit. All the while, our idiotic fowl remained clueless and carried on eating anything that looked like it might be edible. He was like a cartoon character that just couldn't die.

Food was Sean's superpower, but - ultimately - his downfall.

On one fateful sunny Sunday, Darren had hatched his most devious plan yet, hinged largely on wholemeal bread.

At breakfast, he took extra toast, and broke it into tiny pieces, which he filled his pockets with. He snuck into next door's yard, and like a vicious Hansel[264], laid a trail of breadcrumbs from the yard into the road, where he'd laid an infallible trap. The trap was simple but effective; a sheet of wood slathered with glue, and baited with a small pile of bread. Sean predictably toddled straight over to the board, ate the bread and realised that he couldn't get away. This was Darren's chance to shine.

He dragged the sheet of wood away to a quiet corner of his own garden, and marvelled at the opportunities before him. He could staple Sean's wings to the board. He could throw stones at him and there would be no way for Sean to dodge them. He could string him up in the tree or watch him

---

[263] Not **actual** missiles, although Darren would have relished the opportunity to obliterate a small town, given the opportunity   . He really was vile.

[264] He probably would have murdered Gretel in a heartbeat...

starve, he could drown him in paint him or drive over him with the lawnmower. So many choices.

While he plotted, Darren went back into the house and played innocently with some toys, thus reinforcing his parents' firm belief that he was the perfect child. They watched proudly as he built a rainforest diorama out of proprietary building blocks, complete with toucans, monkeys and a butterfly. "Awwwww", they said. "Isn't he clever?", they said. "Wouldn't hurt a fly!", they said.

All the while, Sean was straining to grab flies out of the air as they flew past. He picked off stray bits of bread from his feathers. He mistook one foot for a worm, and had a nibble. His lack of intellect meant that this scenario played out several times before he realised that they were his own feet underneath him.

He slept where he stood[265], hungry and scared.

When the sun came up, Darren was ready to spring into action, foiled only by his mum forcing him to get into the bath before school. He got sidetracked trying to drown some rubber ducks, and by the time he was out and dry it was too late to brutally murder Sean. He would have to wait until the end of the day.

In the meantime, Sean's stomach goblins were getting the better of him. In desperation, he attacked his own legs until they were no longer attached to the rest of his body, whereupon he toppled into the still-tacky glue. He wriggled with every ounce of strength he had, essentially pulling himself out of his own feathers.

---

[265] Of course he did. He was stuck to a sheet of plywood.

He was now naked, legless, and still hungry.

By the time Darren arrived to torture and murder our plucky[266] bird, Sean had dragged himself a considerable distance from his dangerously sticky trap, and was frantically digging a hole with his face, hunting for a worm-based main course. Sadly for him, he was also bleeding quite heavily, and Darren watched in horror[267] as Sean pissed on his cornflakes by dying in front of him, entirely of his own accord.

---

[266] ...more pluck**ed** than pluck**y**...

[267] 'Horror' is natively the wrong word. It was more like disappointment.

Chicken Heaven

There were worms.

There were plush chicken houses.

There were neat buckets of dust to bathe in.

There were perfect mounds of fresh fruit, catching the rays of a warm sun on tiny droplets of water.

There were lush patches of grass, intermingled with eminently perchable[268] bushes.

There were tennis balls, a gentle breeze, swings and a cabbage on a string.

All of these things together were absolute heaven to the 13 feathered freaks who stepped out of nothingness and into this vista of pure, unadulterated joy.

We have long established that chickens do not have facial expressions, but if they did then there would be 13 exact replicas of happy confusion.

Charlie walked shakily towards a clear river, which babbled gently next to him. There was a perfect nest for Charlie to climb into. There were zero foxes, and he was quickly lulled to sleep by the water below.

---

[268] Autocorrect tells me that this is another made-up word. This is becoming a habit.

A short distance from the water, there was an assortment of furniture. Henrietta immediately felt safe, fluttering up to the top of first the wardrobe, and then a chest of drawers. Eventually, once she was certain there were no cats around, she crept under the duvet and drifted off into the most comfortable of sleeps.

Idris realised he could fly[269].

There was a small trike, exactly the right size for a Claudia-sized chicken to ride around on. Once she'd had her fill of cycling, a small (and very safe) car appeared, as if by magic.She spent the rest of eternity giving rides to her friends.

Ken found himself in a weird version of reality, in which anything even slightly phallic was blurred out. He never saw a penis again. He was not alone in this censored version of reality, and was joined by Erica, who was similarly joyful at the prospect of a cockless life.

Nyle walked into his own personal study equipped with a powerful (and largely voice-controlled) computer so that he could write forever more, inspired by the life stories of those around him.

---

[269] Not exactly 'fly' in the truest sense of the word, but it was close enough to make him feel like he was in heaven, which was handy.

Brian and Betty walked wing in wing[270] through lush green countryside, the wind ruffling their feathers and the sun on their wings. Incest is perfectly normal in chickens but a long way from normal in humans, which was a moral dilemma that neither of them realised they were battling with. They were never parted again.

Robin became aware that he had significantly larger (and stronger) wings. One little flap took him effortlessly into the air, where he flapped deftly between the trees and dive-bombed worms to his heart's content. He learned to roost up high, did aerial tricks and became a lovable nuisance.

Astrid was wearing a tiny deer-stalker and a tweed cape. People clucked questions at her and she always seemed to be able to answer them. She found things, solved mysteries and reunited lost, dead, chickens with other lost, dead, chickens. Every day was a success and she seemed to have mastered the art of text-to-speech technology so never again had to use her beak to dial a number.

Ivan was the most bad-ass child minder that Heaven had ever seen. He looked after his growing brood of undead chicks with unprecedented care and nobody fucked with his chicks. He was both the most loving and murderiest[271] chicken guardian in the history of chicken guardians and he

---

[270] This is technically impossible as wings have no fingers and therefore can't possibly hold on to anything. They can, however, touch against each other in what people might refer to as a 'romantic gesture'. This is chicken Heaven; they can do whatever the Hell they like. Without the 'Hell' part, unless Hell is in fact their Heaven. How does that work??

[271] Another made up word. To be fair to Ivan, his murdering was at an all-time low and is generally frowned upon in Heaven, as far as I am aware.

had clearly found his niche in the world. He snuggled, preened fed and entertained his clucky charges for the rest of eternity and almost never ripped any mammalian[272] throat out again.

Norah was a superhero. Like Robin, she was granted the gift of flight in the afterlife and her bright blue and forever clean cape fluttered behind her in perfect form. She never did any particularly good deeds and had no other 'super' traits but she was living her best ~~life~~ death and entertained the youngsters as she darted between the trees and somersaulted through the air. She was super-cool, which was plenty good enough for her.

Sean entered the hereafter with more braincells than he had left his earthly life. He was now into double figures, and generally safe unaccompanied. His happiness was assisted by the lack of evil children[273] aching for his downfall. His ever after was punctuated by as many worms as any chicken could want; warm, juicy and wriggly but not so wriggly that they could escape.

Chicken Heaven is much like human Heaven, but with less white stuff and more invertebrates. Alectryon was a bit of a 'dude' and often strutted amongst his charges,

---

[272] It's important to be specific…

[273] The delightful Darren lived to adulthood, but suffered from a propensity for avian flu and spent a deliciously long period of time in intensive care. Alectryon was a vengeful god; it was not accident that the feather in Darren's blueberry muffin was **almost** big enough to choke on. The salmonella poisoning was serendipitous, as was the chicken-induced road accident. Karma is a bitch.

discussing[274] their existences and demises. When a deceased clucker needed something, Alectryon clicked his/her[275] fingers[276] and there it (whatever 'it' happened to be) was, as long as it sat within the parameters of Chicken Nirvana.

And there we have it. A stupid end, to a stupid story, about a whole load of very stupid chickens.

---

[274] This is Chicken Heaven. Anything is possible, even casual discussion.

[275] Who cares? It's not like there was any procreation on the cards, and who cares what colour 'God' is wearing? In fact, let's face it, who cares what colour **anyone** is wearing??

[276] These are metaphorical fingers. It is impossible to click feathers because they'd only ever make a 'ffft' noise, which is hardly likely to grant any wishes at all.

Postscript

Astrid and Ivan had Special Cuddles several times during their eternity[277] in chicken heaven. Since there is no particular reason why biology should cease to function in the foreverafter, it seems likely that this would result in Astrid begetting mini Astrids. If this is the case, and heaven is a perfect place (without predators), then it would surely be over-run very quickly. Having said that, it is also probably an infinite afterlife, which means there would be an infinite amount of space for an infinite amount of chickens. If heaven can only be populated by entities that have ceased to exist, then only chickens can possibly go to heaven; they have to live before they can die. I think that means that the chicken **has** to come before the egg, although I have to confess that I neither understand nor entirely remember the logic that lead me to that conclusion. Have I just accidentally solved one of the biggest philosophical questions of all time? Shit. I didn't mean to...

---

[277] Eternity is, by definition, a Very Long Time.